PENGUIN BOOKS
UNQUIET HEART SOLILOQUY

Dano Chow is hopeful. He was born in 1990 in Batu Pahat, Malaysia and he has an MA in Philosophy and Contemporary Critical Theory from the Centre for Research in Modern European Philosophy (CRMEP). *Unquiet Heart Soliloquy* is his debut novel.

Unquiet Heart Soliloquy

Dano Chow

PENGUIN BOOKS

An imprint of Penguin Random House

PENGUIN BOOKS

USA | Canada | UK | Ireland | Australia
New Zealand | India | South Africa | China | Southeast Asia

Penguin Books is part of the Penguin Random House group of companies
whose addresses can be found at global.penguinrandomhouse.com

Published by Penguin Random House SEA Pvt. Ltd
9, Changi South Street 3, Level 08-01,
Singapore 486361

First published in Penguin Books by Penguin Random House SEA 2023
Copyright © Dano Chow 2023

ISBN 9789815127058

Typeset in Garamond by MAP Systems, Bangalore, India

www.penguin.sg

For the nobodies

When Orpheus descends towards Eurydice, art is the power by which night opens. Because of art's strength, night welcomes him; it becomes welcoming intimacy, the harmony and accord of the first night. But it is toward Eurydice that Orpheus has descended. For him Eurydice is the furthest that art can reach. Under a name that hides her and a veil that covers her, she is the profoundly obscure point toward which art and desire, death and night, seem to tend. She is the instant when the essence of night approaches as the other night.

—Maurice Blanchot

Contents

Contents

Chapter 1

The term 'Zhongguoren' was historically used to refer to any one person of the Chinese diaspora, irrespective of the dynasty, ruling party or nation state they were born into. But, in the modern times of a globalized Chinese presence, calling someone Zhongguoren could possibly elicit the same hostile response as though you had just called the person a dog-eating Chinaman. Just the other day, I saw a video post on Facebook shaming *daigou* shoppers in Australia for buying more than their allotted quota of baby formula as part of a larger syndicate providing the service of purchasing otherwise unattainable foreign goods on behalf of mainland Chinese buyers, which the daigou would, in turn, resell in China to make a substantial profit. The user who made the post warns the western world, in all caps, that the specific group of Chinese in the video are mainland Zhongguoren. He goes on to make the distinction that they are different from the other Chinese people in Hong Kong, Taiwan, Singapore and Malaysia—a pedantic delineation, I thought, to border on obsession. Surely a hate-filled Neo-Nazi does not stop to consider the diasporic complexities beyond one's skin colour before launching a racist attack? Surely the methods of the daigou who operates purely on a Keynesian model of supply-and-demand are not all that different from the actions of an arbitrager simultaneously buying and selling an asset in different markets, turning a profit that is, in principle, risk free?

As what the Chinese diaspora would call an overseas Chinese person from Malaysia who speaks fluent Mandarin, I wouldn't say I mind all that much when a stranger happens to peg me as a Zhongguoren, for I don't have a problem identifying with the historical usage of the term for a Chinese person, be it an all-encompassing cultural adjective or even when reduced to the less flattering form of the pronoun them. It didn't matter how comfortable I had been in the past about my Chinese identity because the many nuances surrounding the term 'Chinese' became clear to me only after I moved to China. I was born in the 90s and never thought of China as the motherland, but even so I couldn't have foreseen how different it is being Chinese here in China compared to being Chinese in Malaysia, or realized how different being Chinese in China today than from being one before 1989. With such an effervescent culture, China constantly evolves and changes the instant one points to it and thinks they have defined it—this state of flux appearing somewhat capricious, perhaps more so than any other country on earth.

For me, being Chinese in this world was about mastering the art of being in-between.

People often ask me why I came to China, but I don't think any good explanation has ever come from trying to put a visceral impulse into words. Somewhere around the end of last year, I left the year-long summers of Malaysia for the biting cold of Shanghai. Smog had engulfed the entire city during the winter I arrived, an opaque non-organism that would subside intermittently but never completely dissipate, returning relentlessly even through the following spring's transition into summer. All winter a permasmog hung over the city's skyline, mimicking the darkness I harboured within my heart, the very same darkness of which I hoped to be freed when I moved here.

The thing was, my girlfriend, Luna, had gone offline without a trace, and never replied to my calls and messages. I supposed that a long-distance relationship was too much for her, and I was to take it that we were not a thing any more. While all this was happening, my life in Malaysia had become idle from being in a constant state of worklessness, and I guess the choice to major in philosophy—or should I say *not* major in it because I had dropped out of my course—really wasn't the brightest idea I had ever thought of. While I did consider going back to university, I couldn't for the life of me pick something to study, and so I took comfort in worklessness and actually felt quite good not doing anything for a while. Although the hot and humid weather in Malaysia soon got to me and made me increasingly nervous and uneasy, one night, after having *teh tarik* at the *mamak* stall I went home and bought a plane ticket to Shanghai on impulse, almost forgetting that I needed a visa, which I hastily applied for through the travel agency. I packed one carry-on suitcase with whatever meagre winter wear I could find lying around my mother's house, stuffed my laptop into a backpack and converted all my savings into wads of renminbi. Upon inspecting the currency, I was met with the steadfast and approving gaze of Chairman Mao himself, filling me with a weird sense of confidence. I guess I was all set for China.

Arriving in Shanghai was nerve-racking for me at first. I was unable to take in any of the sights and sounds of the city, and immediately sought to find myself a room, a cave to shield myself from the turbulence of the storm around me. I spent a few days gathering my thoughts in a hole at a youth hostel in Jing'An district, before finally taking the plunge to contact Luna. Although she wouldn't answer my calls, I felt a sense of relief when she wrote back. For the first time in a long time, we were texting back and forth just as we used to do. I hoped that she still felt strongly about me, as it hadn't been that long since we had supposedly broken up, but then part of me knew that it was possible that she was replying out of courtesy or from her shock to discover that

I was now in her country. Where sentimentality is concerned, I was the sort who wore my heart on my sleeve, while she was the distant type especially with matters which she considered trivial. Whenever we had one of those senseless arguments straying beyond the edge of reason, she would just fall silent and let the issue drift into the sweet surrender of nothingness.

Eventually, Luna and I made plans to see each other, plans that for one reason or another never seemed to materialize. Weeks of wallowing in a state of self-pity went by. Before I knew it, my tourist visa for China was expiring and I would need to find a job if I wanted to stay on any longer in Shanghai. Good sense dictated that I give up any hopes of seeing Luna and start looking for the next cheap flight home; but there was a part of me that thought I should stay on just a little longer, a part of me that seemed to have only just become aware of my Chinese-ness and wanted to take full advantage of it now by exploring the vast motherland of my ancestors, not as an outsider but as one who would blend in seamlessly and surreptitiously into my immediate environment. It must have been sentimentality and curiosity that eventually trumped my faculties of reason, and with my breath all foggy under a sycamore in the chill of a winter's night, I decided to stay.

I went for interview after interview but always seemed to draw sceptical responses from the HR. How long will you be staying? Won't there be problems securing a visa? Do you support the One-China principle? I answered as best I could, but most of the companies sent me away with flippant smiles. But things have a way of settling themselves. After I moved to Xuhui, for the sycamore trees and coffee if anything, I eventually found myself doing translation work for a local, social-media company, a job I'd found via an agency for foreigners in Shanghai. Translation was a field with which I'd had some experience in Malaysia and so I was able to provide a good résumé for the agency's referral. Getting into translation again felt quite natural to me, although it wasn't all easy and smooth sailing from the start. I had to adjust to the immense workload and constant worry about my visa as it always seemed there was one issue or another that kept it from being finalized. The only plus side was that the hours were flexible as long as I turned my work in before the deadline, which was a good thing that quickly diminished in value when I found out how abruptly new assignments would appear in my inbox without warning. The pay was nothing to write home about, so much so that after settling the matter of rent and a few good nights out on Yongkang Lu, I was stuck eating *Lao Gan Ma* with rice for the rest of the month.

Still, I was glad how things worked out.

The fact that I spoke both fluent Mandarin and English was paramount to my work and although I handled my assignments well, it was hard to see myself going anywhere fast. The articles I worked on were fast-food and WeChat posts, toilet-seat literature that one mindlessly scrolls through. It wasn't exactly groundbreaking journalism, although I wasn't entirely sure I would prefer to be working on that. On a daily basis, I dealt with the kind of writing which was more or less inconsequential to human existence. If, for some reason, I didn't show up for work one day, having decided on a whim to buy a one-way ticket to Xinjiang in order to visit and write about the various mosques around Kashgar, or the existential slowness of the long, train journey to get there, the translation company could easily replace me with anybody who possessed even a rudimentary proficiency in translating English and Mandarin the very next day. There was a constant flux of talent coming in and going out of Shanghai on a daily basis, and I wasn't foolish enough to consider myself anything special or integral to the company.

I didn't mind the nature of work that felt almost menial at times, but part of me was always looking out for something better.

Isn't that similar to what Luna told me right before things ended between us, that what she needed in her life was not a hot-blooded romance, but someone who was unequivocally better for her?

Chapter 2

Thinking about the past and the way everything happened always gave me a headache.

I kept to myself during my first few months in Shanghai, where, apart from the minimal amount of socializing that any work entails, I usually wandered around the city alone. Having detested Mandarin lessons when I was a child, they ultimately proved to be very handy for someone now living in China. This greatly impressed some mainlanders, who were awed for no other reason than the fact that I was an overseas Chinese who spoke their language; and when they learnt that Malaysia was the only country in the world outside of China with its own Chinese education system, it only added to their high esteem of me.

But somehow my days went by in a conflicted state of both fascination and annoyance at the Chinese culture. The fabric of things in my daily life appeared in a state of foreign yet grotesque familiarity. In Malaysia we were not shy to eat well, but not to the point of wastage as in China. When we toasted each other back home, it was symbolic and not because we wanted the other to down their drink in one great gulp. We also loved clothing, shoes and anything to do with the latest trends in fashion just as much as the mainlanders did, but never consumed so much as to make showcasing a certain kind of lavish lifestyle a necessity.

On the pretext of delving deeper into my curiosity about sociological norms in China, I started to use various dating apps to get to know women of my age in Shanghai. The process was a little awkward for me at first as I found myself scrolling through my camera roll, picking out pictures in which I was better-looking, then writing ostentatious descriptions of myself in order to present a likeable sense of self, if I actually had one. I tried not to overdo it at first, but, after spending a few hours swiping left and right, I began to see the lighter side of things. For the most part, most users on the app weren't looking for anything too serious, and those who were, either never wrote back or would readily 'unmatch' and delete you for seeming too eager.

My first few dates (or 'meet ups' as they were called on the app) were fairly casual and typical of a mid-spring outing. Usually, we went out for lunch or coffee to somewhere hip like Wukang Lu, followed by brisk walks around the French Concession, taking our time, not really talking about anything of real importance whilst admiring the lush crispness of the sycamore. We would exhaust the topics of our favourite spots to eat, the cultural differences between the global Chinese diaspora and mainland China, and also places we'd been to and others we hoped to visit someday. Some would talk about their past loves, sentimental reveals they hoped to leave behind with the changing seasons. I wasn't one to talk about myself with great enthusiasm so, when prompted, I recounted with some difficulty the few laughable loves I had experienced during my university life, doing my best to keep the conversation going lest my date discovered that I was actually an exceptionally boring human being. If we weren't too tired after all that and if we felt particularly spontaneous, we'd catch a movie, spending a couple of hours watching some Chinese chick flick that I wasn't sure why I enjoyed. As opposed to being out in the open and walking wherever we pleased, spending time in the confined spaces of a cinema with an almost complete stranger of the opposite sex calmed me. It didn't make me feel as apprehensive as I thought it would, and I only hoped that my dates felt the same way.

Over the course of many Tinder and Tantan dates, I never once brought up my whole situation with Luna; about how I had moved to China only with the hope that I could see her. There was little distance between these raw and undigested emotions and myself. I wasn't eager to reveal what had happened with Luna, for fear that my laying out of the plain facts in front of someone would be entirely underwhelming and thus appear completely disingenuous when taken at face value. The women I went out with probably sensed that I was holding something back and although they did not pry into the matter, it was probably why some of them never went out with me again. When I wrote, they would say they were busy, or they simply didn't reply at all—the latter was more often the case.

On one fine spring evening, I made plans to get drinks on Yongkang Lu with a young lady named Sofia whom I'd met through Tinder. On her profile was the one-liner: *24-year-old Chinese architect from Germany. Modern art over contemporary, studying all things Shanghai!*

In her uploads was a picture of her posing on the Bund, wearing a slightly oversized blazer over a white linen shirt, with plaid slacks and thin-strapped sandals, and then a second one, a flash photograph of her in a fedora, drinking a full goblet of doppelbock at a party.

Cute, I thought.

There wasn't all that much to go on solely based on her profile but, after we chatted, it soon became apparent that we had taken a liking to each other.

Sofia and I both used free VPN apps to circumvent China's firewall, which effectively made the struggle of messaging each other over an unstable connection to a foreign server more difficult, and far less espionage than it actually sounds to be. Finally, after several sporadic flurries of small talk and nonchalant flirting through text, we agreed to meet one Saturday night near

Dapuqiao Station where the narrow streets were invariably full of Chinese youngsters on the parental dole. Immediately, I saw the appeal for Sofia and I to be out there in this crowd, among the lovers and young revellers who were all buzzed up with alcohol and cigarettes. We would be two foreigners in modern China, making face-to-face acquaintance for the first time, having a good time in each other's tipsy company, casually confiding any pent-up frustrations accumulated during the week in the open arms of an online date.

But, when Saturday evening came around, the weather got abnormally hot and my whole body began to brim with unease. To save on rent, I had taken the cheapest studio apartment, facing west, a tiny hole of a place that was like an oven on slow cook against the evening sun. My yellowing air conditioner made the heat bearable but that evening it stalled for a long time, signalling that its days were numbered as it had done many times before. I had already had it serviced a few times since I moved in and although I wasn't a particularly skilled handyman, I was tempted to have a go at it myself if only to put it out of its misery.

I walked over to open the windows, immediately catching a whiff of the pollen carried by the wind. Why was it so hot today? I wondered as I bit the end of a Liqun cigarette from the gold-and-red pack that gleamed brilliantly in the twilight. Its taste profile was heavier with more of a body than your typical Chinese cigarette which, by my logic, made me smoke less even though every puff probably killed you twice as fast. The colleague from Hangzhou, who had given me a pack to try out, had told me that it was all they ever smoked over there in Zhejiang province. I had hated it at first but, over the course of a few months spent smoking with my colleagues outside the office, the brand had grown on me, and I started to care less about whether I actually liked smoking and focused solely on administering myself that small dosage of something strong at the end of each day.

I mulled things over and thought about Sofia, exhaling cigarette smoke as I watched the peak-hour traffic grind to a standstill outside, where only the electric scooters continued to whizz by on the special, side lane assigned to two-wheelers. Back home in Malaysia, the changing of the traffic signal from red to green during peak hour hardly signified anything, and one could very well work through several chapters of a book during the slow crawl home; whereas in Shanghai, you could at least see the long streams of traffic being systematically broken up and its flow regulated by the traffic lights.

Every so often a Didi car would stop to let a passenger on, cueing in a chorus of car horns sounding out across the boulevard.

The hot evening wind blew by. And with that, my scheduled meeting with Sofia that night no longer felt right. It wasn't so much that it felt *wrong* by any means—after all she was friendly and nice enough when we texted online—it's just that part of me couldn't see anything happening with her in the immediate and foreseeable future, not that I knew why this was suddenly important to me. Say, even if we did hit it off and became really into each other right from the start—then what?

A sense of dread and emptiness overwhelmed me. One last drag from the cigarette, wondering what I could tell Sofia to get her to agree to postpone our date.

The sun was setting, and I was running out of time. I picked up my phone, only to close the WeChat app as soon as I had tapped on it. The temperature in my room had risen since the air conditioner shut down, and so I naturally opened the Waimai app to order a bowl of *Liang ban mian* and beer from a nearby eatery. The process of browsing and ordering Waimai would happen instinctively for me, as was my customary cigarette whilst waiting for the deliveryman downstairs (I never had them come up). On this day, it took him ten minutes to deliver, a few minutes short of the record, and in no time, I polished off the cold noodles and lit a cigarette as dessert to go with the beer.

I didn't see Sofia that night. I told her that I was behind with a work deadline and needed to cancel. She said she understood and that it wasn't a problem; so I never quite understood her reason for blocking me after that.

And that was that.

Sunken way down in the dregs of my memory was that smoky June night, at the turn of spring into summer, of the sharp, cracking sounds of plastic Waimai packaging, breaking into transparent shards that tore through the paper bag as I forced it deeper into the overflowing rubbish bin.

Chapter 3

The company that I worked for was called *TRIESTE* (*deliyasite* in Mandarin), a dedicated social-media press that was founded some five years ago. With the help of its HR, I managed to secure a year-long work visa that would last me until just about the end of next winter; and with that out of the way, I spent my first official month on the company payroll dealing with an ever-increasing workload.

After starting me off easy, the editor gradually assigned me more pieces with every successful translation I submitted to a point where it became quadruple the amount that a translator would be tasked with in Malaysia. I wasn't sure if anyone else noticed the effort I put into my translations, but the feedback from the editor seemed positive and genuine enough, because she soon assigned me translations covering topics that were more cultural and engaging to both readers and translator, ranging everywhere from travel and leisure to real-estate and entertainment.

This new challenge was fresh, but not altogether fun for me. With the more interesting articles came an increased sense of responsibility towards each phrase and mannerism that made up a coherent translation. A lot of my time was spent in dealing with the many colloquialisms and expressions that were simply untranslatable from Mandarin to English, and vice versa.

'Take it easy,' the editor would tell me. 'The readers don't expect a perfect, word-for-word translation seeing that most of them don't pay attention to the fact that the writing is translated in the first place anyway,' she laughed. 'You know, every translation done well constitutes a classic in itself, so give every sentence room for deviation from the original writing. Try to have fun with it.'

She was right, the act of translating did feel like creating one's very own brainchild and I didn't think of it as merely interpreting one language to another. Since coming here, I experienced translation happening within the same Mandarin language shared across the greater Chinese diaspora: where in China 'paying the bill' means paying the bill, in Malaysia we say we 'give back money'; and hot water in China means hot water, but in Malaysia we refer to it as 'burning water'; and in China a biscuit goes soft from moisture in the atmosphere, but in Malaysia it merely 'loses its air'; and last but not least, in China people chit-chat but in Malaysia people 'blow water'. The language of the Nanyang has long deviated from that of the language in China and for that reason there was many a time when I felt that whatever I said in my accented Mandarin would sound like a bad translation— and that I would only exist in China as a bad translation.

As I was translating into English, the subtle differences in Mandarin were negligible for the most part, and I was quick to learn the ropes and operate like a machine, churning out copy after copy whenever it was asked of me.

'You're too good at your job,' the editor said one day, after inviting me into her office, not bothering to offer me a coffee or a seat on the stained, velvet chair I pulled gingerly towards me.

'You're no *shabi*. You know very well I didn't invite you here this morning to praise you,' she paused, first, to light a cigarette and second, to puff and exhale. 'The speed at which you work is making us Zhongguoren look bad. Aren't you folk from the Nanyang supposed to be more laid back, and not work with such machine-like efficiency?'

The editor was thirty-five years old but could've easily passed for somebody in her mid-twenties. According to the grapevine in the office, she had founded the company at the age of thirty, was single, independently wealthy and lived alone. At her birthday party that year, we bought her a first edition Hemingway (supposedly her favourite writer), only to discover that she already owned several in mint condition.

I wasn't sure if the editor was actually expecting a response from me, so I waited for her to go on. The air in the old office room was musty and dank with the funk of cigarettes, probably from all of those smoked since way back in the days of economic reform. The editor was smoking a pack of Zhonghua, which she eventually passed my way.

I obliged.

'Some of us aren't as lazy, *laoban*,' I said, exhaling after a long draw.

She brought up my file, her eyebrows raised and her lips curled in irony. Then a warm smile broke through although I could never guess what she was thinking; perhaps it was the nicotine kicking in. I knew she wasn't going to switch up her view of Southeast Asians just yet, which was good for me, because I remained an anomaly in her eyes for now. In the editor's mind, I was probably one of the slightly overachieving Nanyang Chinese, who were supposed to be lazier than the other 1.3 billion Chinese in this world—how nice.

'This is what we're going to do. I don't want to waste your proficiency with language, so I'm transferring you to journalism where you'll be . . . covering the latest fashion trends for starters. Best not to squander your linguistic talent doing good English translations of mediocre Chinese articles, not when you can be producing great, and let's even say unique and original, pieces for our English readers, right?'

I wanted to be flattered but knew that what this really meant was that I would now be saddled with both translating work and writing work. At the end of the day, I didn't really care what I was assigned to do, so I simply continued to smoke the red Zhonghua cigarette in silence, the taste of history coursing through every fibre of my being.

And that was that.

I sent off my translation proofs for the week and was almost immediately assigned, via email, my very first assignment to cover a story on fashion the next day. It felt odd reading the brief, knowing that I wasn't required to translate anything, which had become second nature to me, be it purely as a job or as an art form if you will. In any case, I needed to look forward now. When I had needed a job to stay in China, I had told myself that I would accept anything that came my way, and my motto hadn't really changed. Now I had to re-focus on the next task: writing.

The art of writing was something I had never really taken seriously before, save a few pseudo-radical pieces that tried to express a juvenile disillusionment with the education system, that I remember penning so fervently for my high school magazine back in the day, only for the piece to be perfunctorily accepted and then scrapped by the board of student editors. I couldn't blame them; they were friendless, and I wasn't very good.

Now having just gotten into the flow of translation work, all of a sudden I was set on the path of writing for TRIESTE. The editor boss seemed immensely wealthy, and the company was doing very well under her helm, which made it unlikely that I was just filling in as a cost-cutting move, for she could have easily had head-hunters bring in some budding writers next Monday.

Did she see something special in me which she wanted to unveil? That precise something which Luna had so casually dismissed?

Chapter 4

Dear Luna,

Have you been well? I hope business has been good for you in Wenzhou.

Things have been good with me. I've been kept busy with work. As of today, I am no longer a translator but a writer. I am not entirely sure how I feel about the change right now, but my gut feeling is that it will take me somewhere someday. China has already given me so much over the past few months.

When can I see you?

I hope I'm not out of line for asking you this after everything that has happened.

I do miss talking to you. Every day. All the time. I find myself thinking of you. Things were so different then because we were together. When you left, you gave me the motivation to work hard and the desire to find and stick with a vocation that falls in line with what I feel comfortable with in this world. I've thought long and hard since we last talked and have tried to look at my existence without prejudice, effectively isolating my being from this shell. This of course isn't possible, but wouldn't that be something? To contemplate my existence from outside of myself? How much easier would every decision be then?

All my life I've found myself to be less of an outsider in the Camusian sense, and more of an in-betweener who hovers in and out of existence on the fringes of community. As you know, I'm a Han Chinese whose mother tongue is English, who then studied Mandarin and Malay in school. Who could've foreseen that these language skills would come in handy? If I had never come to China to look you up, I might have never discovered any use for language beyond everyday conversation.

Do wish me well. Coming here has really given me a new lease of life I'm much grateful for.

Please write to me sometime.

I want to hear from you again.

I smoked one more cigarette to unwind, and then sent the message to Luna. It was past midnight, and she was probably asleep by now. It wasn't like I expected her to write back anyway.

I got up at 5 a.m. the next morning, earlier than I usually would so that I would have ample time to smoke, wash up and get to Huaihaizhong Lu well before the doors opened at Nike.

Today, I was covering a release of a limited-edition sneakers. My MO (modus operandi) was for me to arrive at sunrise to survey the demography of the people in the queue, photograph and hopefully interview a few of them to shed some light on their passion for sneakers and the necessary sacrifices in sustaining this expensive interest.

Following my briefing with the editor, I had a rudimentary framework in mind for the scoop she sought. Some time ago, mob violence had broken out in Asia due to the inadequate supply of the Adidas NMD—a lifestyle sneaker so comfortable it had masses of people pitching camp at the shopping-mall entrances on the eve of its release. The editor had completely disregarded the story at the time as she had simply dismissed it as kids rioting over luxury goods marketed in limited quantities. To her, the story was merely a 21st century capitalistic tale of scarcity marketing; but then it took her by surprise that the hysteria surrounding these unrests was not endemic to China alone but part of a larger global streetwear scene that was completely new to her. This was very much a niche scene, where hobbyists hustled out of necessity to further fund their addiction for shoes. The resellers who made a killing on this decided to make this their full-time job, and the editor saw the potential for a unique story to be told through the world of streetwear-and-sneaker culture. I was to give her this story.

I showered and left my apartment, lit another cigarette and made my way south towards Huaihaizhong Lu. I hadn't been up this early in a while, and the crisp morning air made me feel very guilty for smoking. The first smoke of the day against the rising sun, all that was missing now was a steaming cup of *kopi-o*. I took a short drag and spat. God, it sure felt good to spit sometimes.

I was running a little late and ended up getting on a rental Mobike, only stopping briefly for some *baozi* and soy milk on my way there. I was still new to the whole concept of renting a bicycle via the scanning of QR codes and I would often forget that this was a legitimate means of transport available to me. When I did remember I could use a Mobike, my navigation of the two-wheeler was slow and awkward as I was overwhelmed by the sheer numbers of riders on the road, not to mention having to cycle on the right side of the road rather than left.

But, being up this early meant that there was hardly any traffic on the road and I was nearing Nike in no time. I parked the Mobike at one of the nearby racks and walked the rest of the way, taking my sweet time with the baozi and soy milk, now at perfect drinking temperature after the short ride.

I lit another cigarette and fished out my phone.

Luna hadn't texted back; I realized the message had failed to send.

I first got to know Luna two years ago. And if I could only reverse that right-swipe on her profile I would do it in a heartbeat.

She was twenty-one with bluish hair at the time, a Wenzhou native who loved fashion and with a bottomless bank account. She was beautiful and nice—what more can I say?

We matched on the Tantan app when she was in Malaysia, during one of the many trips her family took together throughout the year. It didn't matter the budget, distance, or time of year.

It could be the Swiss alps, the Milford Sound, or the Machu Picchu ruins—just as long as there were no visa complications, they would go.

Back then, her family had hired a guide from one of the top tour companies to take them around Malaysia in a Mercedes Sprinter, and so her replies were sporadic, often only to ask what was good to eat or to complain about local hygiene and the overall laid-back nature of good Malaysian folk.

How on earth had I become so smitten, let alone decide to start an online relationship with her in such a short span of time?

The change of seasons brought on a peculiar melancholia I had never felt before. It was subtly different from the heat back home, which was a year-long constant, as was to be expected from one humid hell on the edge of the equator. Here, the sadness that underpins the heatwaves peculiar to summer tends to propagate itself throughout the longer days of the season and culminates in a blue funk in the hottest and most unbearable of afternoons. When I watched the setting sun drop from its zenith into the horizon that evening, with its rays piercing through the leaves of the sycamore to turn all life underneath it a brilliant gold, I felt an immense relief, like I had made the right choice for the first time in my life.

I spent the entire afternoon at a café, carefully selecting and editing the pictures from the sneaker drop, then compiling the notes I had taken during my interviews to form a short but concise article. Time flew by as I wrote and the process didn't feel all that different from working on a translation. I worked with the same quick sandwich and the same savourless coffees, left at the same 5 p.m. I never left after it got dark, I found it a little too depressing.

I lit a cigarette and thought about my day.

Covering my first story was not as fun as I had hoped it would be. Nothing out of the ordinary had happened on the job. There had been no eureka moments to kick start the writing. No fights in the queue to commemorate my first day as I had desired.

It was utterly ordinary, just as my life had been so far.

But then I heard someone calling my name.

Someone was saying my name from behind me, a deep voice from another realm, reverberating through the calm summer evening.

I turned around to come face to face with a woman who looked like she had stepped out of the pages of *Vogue*, in her oversized, Comme des Garçons, graphic tee, plaid culottes and brogues.

Before I could register how well-thought-out her outfit was, she'd already clouted me hard across the head with what I later found out was a Dongbei Jiaoziguan waimai box.

My cigarette butt flew out of my lips, trailing an arc of wispy smoke as it fell to the concrete.

'I knew it was you! That's for blowing me off the other night you greasy man!'

I probably had that one coming, nevertheless I was a little taken aback at having been assaulted with hot dumplings of all things, which fortunately escaped damage as I'm not sure what she would have done then. *Greasy* sounded so original and entirely befitting a description of me that I had to hand it to her.

'Pleasure to finally meet you, Sofia,' I said, offering her a cigarette.

Chapter 5

It didn't take too long for Sofia to get her point across, to establish in no uncertain terms that she was a feminist. Yes, I was aware that she had her own cigarettes and didn't need to get them from any man (the antagonist role which I had assumed by default simply because I was born with a penis). I was also aware that I ought not to have blown her off or have 'given her the pigeon' as the Chinese would say; perhaps then she wouldn't feel the need to admonish me for being so ill-mannered. However, I couldn't fathom why she had blocked me willy-nilly on the app, without even giving me a chance to explain myself or make it up to her. In fact, considering that it had all happened quite some time ago, why was she still mad about it?

A strong, independent woman needs no shoulder to lean on. But the same can be said for any strong, independent person, who may be stronger still for knowing that they needn't flaunt their strength to the world. I thought better against telling her this for fear that it would fan her flames and push her over the edge.

We must have chain-smoked what felt like five cigarettes as she bellyached incessantly about God alone knows what. My throat was dry and I was absolutely famished, so I asked Sofia whether she would like to join me for some crab noodles before I succumbed to the insidious thought of stealing her dumplings.

'You're kidding,' she scoffed. 'And what am I supposed to do with my dumplings?'

'We'll eat it on the side. Come on. It's my treat.'

We walked on in silence, watching the stain trail of the setting sun like blots of crimson ink diffusing through the horizon.

Sofia had neither accepted nor rejected my dinner invite, but she at least let me light her cigarette for once without bringing up women's suffrage.

'You're going in the wrong direction, we're going to Sinan Lu,' she said.

'Are we visiting the Sinan Mansions?'

'Don't be silly. We're going there because the best place to get crab noodles is Sinan Lu.'

'I like the one on Huaihaizhong Lu. Plus, it's closer to my place.'

'Well, the one on Sinan Lu is closer to where I stay, so we're going there,' she said. 'Besides, what does a foreigner know about where to eat? All you guys ever eat is waimai from the most overhyped dianping listings.'

There wasn't much I could say to refute that. But hang on . . .

'Wait . . . aren't you from Europe? Although I must say you're pretty spot on with the local southern Chinese accent . . .'

'What are you, the police?' she retorted.

I held my peace, took another drag and exhaled. The sky was almost completely dark now.

'I'm from here, but moved around a lot when I was younger, is that good enough? Now, no more questions until we get food, otherwise, I won't let you buy me dinner,' she said, trotting on ahead of me in her fancy-dress shoes.

What does someone say to that?

We ate with gusto that night.

Sofia was right, the crab noodles was indeed far better in this hole-in-the-wall joint on Sinan than the kind they served up in my usual eatery. We had worked up a good appetite by the time we were done with all the walking, and beer was the ideal drink to cool off and unwind at the end of a hot day.

We ate, drank, smoked and polished off the box of dumplings with which Sofia had beaned me, and then smoked again.

She didn't eat that many of her own dumplings; in fact, it seemed like she didn't fancy the stuffed medallions of chive and pork at all, so I scarfed them down with some vinegar from the noodle store. She must've really loved the crab noodles.

Sofia seemed to be in a better mood now that her belly was full and she wasn't running on nicotine fumes, but I still refrained from asking why she had been so upset as to throw a mini tantrum, involving steaming hot dumplings. She was back to her usual self—if I could be so bold as to claim to know her that well—and I was now asking what cigarettes she preferred, refilling her glass of Qingdao after she emptied it. Any qualms we might've had about each other were now gone. It was like meeting up with an old friend you never knew that well, who actually turned out to be fun.

After eating our fill of yellow noodles and downing half a dozen Qingdao each, we were somewhat given to the sense of lightness permeating the summer's night and in the hope of chasing the distant scent of rain and petrichor carried in all its purity by the warm August breeze, we resumed our walk.

An unconscious decision took us south where, two cigarettes later, was the Dapuqiao residential district and the Tianzifang shikumen. Somehow, we had managed to make it to where we had initially planned to meet some months ago, albeit indecorously loud and sozzled.

She wanted ice cream, so I got her ice cream at a roadside stall.

Then she wanted more beer and thought it was a good idea to ask the ice cream server for some.

'No beer here!' the waiter ejaculated in frustration.

I laughed. Was I out of cigarettes already?

She tried again, this time in pseudo-German English instead, *'Komm on, ja, I vil trade you zis pox of Meffius for ein bier. Okay?'*

The waiter gave me a speaking look. I only just met her, man!

'I hate this I hate this I hate this,' she mumbled as I pulled her away.

'Relax. So, we'll get beer somewhere else.'

'No! You don't get it at all . . . Aaaaaa! Let's go get some *jianbing*.'

'You can still eat?'

'Shut up! I didn't eat much all day. You're still buying, right?'

Traditionally from Tianjin in the north, jianbing was now a street delicacy ubiquitously available throughout China, although they don't quite make it the same way as they do in Shanghai, Sofia explained. This particular stall which we went to was manned by a spirited youth with nothing but a grill and an assortment of condiments on his bike. The queue for his product was a long one, primarily made up of budding university graduates. Sofia told me that the draw was because of the *sunshine boy* look he sported with his mono eyelids and clean-shaven face.

'Testosterone and pheromones, a solid foundation for any *Weishang* business.'

'Shut up . . . it's because he makes it the proper Tianjin way, using only mungbean, crispy *guobier*, green onion and nothing else.'

'I bet he adds some special sauce too,' I argued.

'*Xiaogege*, could we get two jianbing? With extra sauce and green onion,' she said when we finally reached the front of the queue, sounding the sweetest she had all night.

See? Extra sauce.

'I'm stuffed. Why don't you get just one?'

'I'm not sharing with you! Get your own!' she squeaked, almost breaking into falsetto.

Even Xiaogege shook his head. Sofia could hardly contain her excitement.

I paid and collected the two steaming pancakes from the sunshine boy. His eyes did glitter a little.

Chapter 6

We found ourselves on a steel bench, depleted not only of our cigarettes but also of the desire to go beyond the first few bites of our piping hot wraps. We were a couple who had been left behind by the passing moment. Only when the high had died down did the utter ridiculousness of the entire evening dawn on us.

I thought about calling it a night and heading home to proofread the article I had worked on all afternoon. But Sofia was tugging gently at my shirt and asking me if I would like to go up to her place for some more beer. I wasn't entirely sure what she meant by this, but when I asked her if she was interested in reading my article, she didn't seem all that set against the idea.

She asked me if I wanted any more cigarettes. I shook my head.

'Thank God,' she sighed.

'Tell me more about the things you hate,' I said, as we spooned in bed, my arm wrapped around her body, my face buried in her back.

I brought my hand up stealthily to rest on her breasts, where I could feel the soothing undulations of her breathing. She was quiet, and for a moment I thought she had drifted off to sleep; but then she turned around and pulled herself closer to me. With her eyes shut she seemed to mull over the question for a while, as if she were pondering the essence of being itself.

'I hate this furry chest hair of yours that grows in random wisps and . . . and that streetwear article you made me read!' she whispered.

That hurt, even though she was supposed to be kidding. My disappointment must have been evident, me never being able to suppress my emotions. She must've somehow sensed this because she started caressing my face. She opened her eyes, her gaze bright in the semi-darkness around us and proceeded to kiss me passionately, all the way from my lips down to my sparsely haired chest.

We tried to give it another go.

Still nothing. Not a damned thing. I just couldn't get it up.

'It's fine . . . you're just a bit tired today,' she said, her breath no longer short and heavy.

Her hand touched my face, I continued staring straight up into space.

The temperature from the day had finally eased off and a cool breeze wafted in through mosquito netting fitted in her windows. The only shapes I could discern in the darkness were the wind chimes, made of scrap aluminium, producing a faint tinkling sound in the draught, and the contours of her bedside-table clock ticking away the early morning seconds with its measured hands.

She wriggled free from my embrace and turned away, flicking on a soft-yellow light to illuminate her bedroom. The accordion sconce on her side of the bed cast a shadow of her figure on the wall and as my eyes adjusted to the light, I could make out her finely sculpted shoulder blades, and what looked like a Scorpio zodiac sign tattooed in cubist form; it appeared to be juggling roses between its pincers.

In the dim lighting her room appeared minimal, but in reality it was just devoid of objects. There was no clutter, with only a few traces here and there of Sofia living in this space. A pen and concealer the only colonizers of the kitchen counter, books and loose sheets of paper strewn all across the white standing desk, a linen shirt hanging on the wall. On the dresser was a silver camera alongside two big plastic bags, containing, I presumed, film canisters. The space hadn't been renovated and wasn't particularly homey, although it was evidently very well thought out, exuding a unique charm brought out by the individuals who were both the designer and inhabitants of that space. The apartment was austere, but messy enough in places that it offered an aesthetic with Sofia's own authenticity to it.

She reached for her panties lying on the parquet floor and after putting them on, lit up another cigarette. She turned around and with an expressionless gaze, simply looked at me.

What was this? I couldn't help but feel utterly naked.

'I should probably get going,' I said, pulling the sheets over my crotch.

'Are you in a hurry to get home? The buses don't start plying for a few hours still.'

Through the tightly fitted, square netting, I peered into the darkness outside—an empty street on the other side of the world in which Sofia and I had dwelt just a few hours ago. The thought of stepping back into that loneliness wasn't all that appealing.

Sofia looked at me, her expression bemused and then indifferent. I couldn't tell if she wanted me to stay or not, what with her staring me down with arms folded over her sullen breasts, their brownish-black teats imploring me to act on what was now turning into protracted indecision.

My mouth was parched—a desert in which I ineffectively searched for words.

She killed the cigarette with a hiss and moved the electric fan to blow a draught in the direction of the window. Then she drew close to me and with her body and full bosom leaning halfway across the bed, blew the last plume of cigarette smoke right into my face.

'Can we just sleep?' I managed to say between coughs.

'I'd like that. You can stay as long as you want.'

After we said our goodbyes the next morning, Sofia quietly disappeared from my life again. I didn't ask for her number, and neither did she remove me from her WeChat blacklist. Like two ships passing in the night, we continued on our separate journeys towards the specific kind of loneliness and space we desired in this world, one that somehow never aligned with the true unloneliness we deserved.

I didn't feel like smoking after that.

It wasn't that I was being overly health conscious nor was I suddenly turned off by the idea of habitually inhaling cigarette smoke to savour the buzz of nicotine coursing through my body. The fact of the matter was, I had quite simply woken up that day completely devoid of any desire to light up.

No. Not one puff.

Didn't want it. Didn't need a cigarette with my morning coffee and *youtiao*—a kind of ritual I had developed since moving to Shanghai. Didn't smoke during my breaks at work either, not even when I went out drinking where I'd usually burn through a pack easy.

Weeks went by, and the odd thing was I didn't feel any healthier, more invigorated or better about myself.

Since it didn't make all that much of a difference, should I smoke again? No. I was certain that I could no longer bear the taste of a cigarette, any cigarette, while back in the day this aversion only applied to menthols which I found wholly revolting. One day, a colleague stuffed a Seven Stars between my lips and lit it, but I gagged, hocked up a loogie and spat it out. It was now an impossibility for me; I could never get beyond the first drag.

Had being with Sofia subconsciously cured me of something; something that had somehow been weighing me down? However, my inability to smoke was beginning to worry me; it was a mystery that intrigued me and not in a small way. Had I gone beyond my limit during that night out with Sofia, causing my body to recoil from nicotine to make up for the heavy toll I'd put it through over the course of the year since I started this habit?

God damn it, I wanted a smoke so bad!

The signs were impossible to read because there were none. What I needed was access to the unconscious signifiers, exclusive to the world of dreams and the suppressed psyche. Cigarettes were bad for me, but even so I had enjoyed them. Could it be that meeting Sofia had blocked off my access to that specific vein of the pleasure principle? If that were the case, what had replaced it?

Whatever it was, it wasn't clear to me. I became deeply depressed because I was no longer able to smoke. No more morning pick-me-ups, nor beautiful moments of sunset nicotine to wind down after the day. It was one less thing to look forward to in the daily grind of my mundane life.

She hadn't responded to any of my messages for a while, but I still thought I should call Luna to talk about this. She had always been fascinated by behavioural changes and I imagined she'd have some light to throw on my predicament.

'It appears that I have stopped smoking,' I said the moment the dial tone faded.

Through the hiss of static on the other end came Luna's voice, fuzzy from the bad connection or the ever-increasing distance between us, I wasn't sure which.

'Oh? That's convenient. Just stop then. You were such a light smoker, I thought you had given up long ago,' she said, in her signature nasally accent.

I told her about how I had just woken up one morning wholly devoid of the desire to smoke.

'It wasn't that I found it difficult to quit before this, I just never felt the need to do so.'

'That's what every smoker says! Especially after smoking so much in one night, you almost had a stroke by the end of it. First comes the creeping worry for your health that I like to call smoker's remorse, and then a lingering sense of guilt—all genuinely felt, but just as easily washed away with a cold shower on Monday morning.'

'But I really have stopped, and I don't know why. I actually do want to smoke again, and I've tried to do so many times! But instead of feeling relief and pleasure, it's revolting. I don't know what's going on.'

'Theoretically, you could, and indeed should, feel some pleasure when you inhale cigarette smoke, even if it's only psychological. Also, still speaking theoretically, you should feel better and healthier ever since you stopped smoking, but the function of theory is not for us to dwell within its domain, leave that to the romantics and the academics . . .'

A faint blowing sound came from her end. I wasn't sure if it was due to bad network coverage, or if she was smoking a cigarette herself.

'. . . don't get confused and feel the need to pinpoint where theories dissolve into actual praxis, okay? You should allow yourself tangents in life.'

Silence. Then there was the sound of gusting wind again. I turned and switched hands, trying to get a better connection.

'Where are you, Luna? I miss you so much.'

'I'm learning to live the existence of a poet.'

'Which one in particular?'

'I like Sappho:

Straightway, a delicate fire runs in
my limbs; my eyes
are blinded, and my ears thunder.
Sweat pours out: a trembling hunts
me down. I grow

paler than grass and lack little of dying.'

'I like it. Send me a link, okay?'

'Sure, but hey, listen . . . there's a lot going on in my life at the moment. I don't even know how to begin telling you.'

My heartbeat quickened, and a sense of uneasiness set in. Our drifting apart from each other was inevitable, but this was the first time it felt real to me.

'Are you back in Shanghai?'

'Yes. I came back quite some time ago.'

'You never said.'

'Well, you didn't ask. And I've been busy.'

'Okay, let me ask you something else. Have lunch with me this weekend.'

I stood there and waited, listening for anything beyond the long, muffled blur of silence emanating from the other end.

'That's not a question, but okay.'

Chapter 7

I dreamt that night that I was in my hometown in Malaysia, not far from the bridge to Singapore. I was drinking *teh tarik* and smoking the very first stick from a red pack of Marlboro.

I was sitting at the entrance of a mamak stall under a curved, perspex awning that pitter-pattered in the rain which was bucketing down relentlessly. Silent lightning flashed in the far distance and there was that unmistakable scent of wet, smouldering asphalt in the night air.

The cigarette seemed to burn endlessly. I sucked on the filter and absorbed drag after drag of nicotine and tar into my body, but it still wouldn't burn out. I tapped and flicked the ash from its tip, but nothing seemed to fall from the burning cherry.

Could this be heaven, or was it hell? I wondered, as I eyed the fresh pack of cigarettes and the eternal cancer stick.

Right, it's Marlboro Red. Of course, it's gotta be hell.

If that were the case, it was truly a pleasant hell, for I had always felt an inimitable sense of calm every time it rained at midnight. In the distance I could see the fluttering of leaves on the branches of the giant ficus tree, ushering in the first droplets of rain by bending its body in an elaborate rain dance. Stray cats and dogs dived for cover and the wild boar retreated to the estates after doing his rounds of scavenging on the roads. There was no traffic in the streets, no stragglers running hunched over, their arms hugging their core protectively from the onslaught of the monsoon pellets. This nocturne was gradually turning into a polonaise, and the rain painted a tranquil scene fit for a most romantic unfolding: suspense in its first percussive moments, soon, each undulation built into a gradual crescendo brought on by the wind until it climaxed into the deafening chorus of a torrential cataract, relentless and brimming with life.

I was hungry in the dream. When I looked down at the steel table, a plate of Hainanese chicken rice had appeared out of nowhere. Try as I might, I was unable to eat it. The dream forbade me from touching the glistening meat.

'Steng, eh?'

I turned and saw the *ah neh* waiter behind me, who made sure I saw him bringing two fingers up to his mouth, in the universal gesture for a smoke. Why would he ask for a half steng, when there was an infinite pack right here?

'You want half? I've been smoking this one for ages. Here!' I moved the red cigarette packet and lighter closer to him, 'Why don't you help yourself to a fresh one?'

'Steng *rokok*, steng, okay?'

I rolled my eyes and passed him my cigarette. Why would he want mine when he could have a whole new one to himself?

I watched as he finished the cigarette, something I had failed to do myself.

'*Tankiu*, boss. Now we make you dream.'

I reached for the pack to light another cigarette, but it was completely empty now.

A dream? Wasn't this one already?

'Tell me what dream you want, I order for you. I order for you now,' he said.

'Food,' I replied, pointing to the chicken rice.

'No meat. Fast you,' he refused. Then he left with an enigmatic shake of his head—I didn't know whether it meant yes or no.

The rain eased up a bit. As the weather got clearer, I was able to make out Singapore in the distance across the bridge, its skyline lit up radiantly. There was no traffic at all, no rush hour at customs with Singaporeans speeding back to Singapore with their tanks full of subsidized RON97 petrol, no Malaysians coming back to Johor with a salary now worth thrice as much as it used to do. I didn't know about 'ordering any dreams', but it would certainly be nice if I could hail a cab now and have the Causeway and clean streets all to myself.

I could get actual edible Hainanese chicken rice at the hawker centres; the Malaysian stuff didn't quite compare.

What was her name again? I could invite her over for the weekend. We could drive over and get lost in the city together as we had always hoped, have mediocre food that was at least healthy and pay way too much for everything.

I found myself standing in the middle of the Causeway with nothing around me but the dark water. At that moment it was not great emptiness that filled me, but a great peace.

Then, the sound of footsteps crept up behind me. I turned around and was met with a majestic tableau.

Marching towards me was a procession of folk worshippers dressed in white robes. They neared me carrying their various gods on wooden, sedan chairs, their movements synchronized as they swayed and chanted in a trance. Each chair was emblazoned with the names of the god or a well-wishing idiom: *Prosperous country, peaceful people! Smooth sailing with the wind! Seasonable weather, timely rains!* These were devout Taoists who surrounded the shamans and priests dressed as the gods they worshipped. They marched alongside those who moved the altars as they danced; and in the darkness the miniature temples and sailboats, decorated with multi-coloured LED lighting, was garish but simultaneously mesmerizing. Then came more devotees, leading the way for the *Jitong* shamans fully enchanted in trance. Shaking their heads, these Jitong mediums were completely being controlled by the forces of the spirit world; despite the repeated flagellation to their flesh, their gaze remained unwavering; their cheeks impaled on steel rods, they continued their macabre dance oblivious to pain.

Heng ah! Huat ah! chanted the Taoists in Hokkien.

A commotion seemed to be breaking out among their ranks, and I nimbly jumped aside to avoid being crushed by the swelling stampede.

Another group came through, bearing a gigantic paper boat. The boat was immense, about twenty metres long and fashioned of ornate ghost paper. It bore the head of a dragon and had a shrine for a body, its lanterns and flags painted with more idioms and the names of the martyred emperor-gods.

Heng ah heng ah heng ah! Huat ah huat ah huat ah!

A thunderous clamour of drums heralded the arrival of the nine gods. The Jitong shamans continued their dance down the Causeway bridge, flogging themselves in self-flagellation. Another group came carrying a sacred urn containing the spirit of the gods on another sedan chair. The more violently it swayed, the more surreal and divine the whole scene became.

I was one with the crowd marching across the vast bridge to Singapore, except it wasn't Singapore which we eventually reached but a sandy shoreline. The wind was muggy and the night humid. The dragonboat was hoisted down the shore, where the shamans continued their ritual dancing and chanting. Lighting joss sticks, hundreds of devotees stopped to kneel and pray. The dragonboat was set on fire signalling the end of the yearly sojourn for the nine star gods of the big dipper. As the flames grew, so did its radiant reflection in the dark waters. The blaze quickened. A film of perspiration coated our bodies beneath our white robes. And the sea. There was the sea. We held aloft the burning boat and trudged across the shore; but before we came to the water, the sand beneath us turned to fiery coal.

Jiu huang da di huat ah huat!

Jiu huang da di huat ah huat!

The worshippers bit back their pain as they continued to chant.

I, on the other hand, was unable to feel anything at all.

Chapter 8

After getting out of the shower on Saturday morning, I spent a great deal of time examining my face in the bathroom mirror, my hair slicked back. Transfixed by my reflection, I remained rooted to the spot, the water trickling from my body and pooling on the mosaic floor at my feet.

My best feature was arguably my prominent cheekbones but, even as I turned my head with my thumb and forefinger spanning my cheeks, I could see that the flesh on my face was beginning to sag. Gone was the chiselled, handsome face of my youth now that the shadows creeping beneath my eyes threatened to develop into bags; they would eventually betray my cumulative unwisdom. I blinked a couple of times and after screwing my eyes shut, I tried opening them as wide as I could, trying to convince myself that inasmuch as I unconsciously squinched, they weren't as small or narrow as people would believe.

What was in the Chinese Zhonghua look to a face anyway? It is in the name of the pursuit for identity that one must first delineate boundaries aiding the sorting of archetypes, so that the said divisive act for the greater good of creating culture is made more convenient for race theory, cultural research and what-have-you. But conversely, in the false actualization of an archetype in the form of a stereotype, the simple mind shrinks these boundaries around the aforementioned archetype before closing it off completely so that any notion that a Chinese person dwells in a world which is in between the universal conception of a race and the specific reality of daily life becomes irretrievably lost.

I really couldn't and didn't want to wrap my head around the topic of Chinese identity. A simple Baidu search of the word Zhonghua, yields images of Zhonghua cigarettes in their classic red packaging, with the gold emblem of Tiananmen Square underneath the traditional Chinese branding—that was my preferred signifier of the loaded term.

I splashed some water on my face and rubbed it gently, trying to exfoliate and clear my pores of any clogging. Then I dug deep into my wide nostrils to remove what seemed to be a primordial piece of mucus. This made me sneeze, and I spat into the sink.

Was I not still handsome? If not as a Chinese, then as a human being? I wondered, patting myself dry with a towel.

The editor had once told me that, as a person advances in age, life has its way of opening up opportunities and pathways to the greater plateaus untraversed, and so there's less of a need to compensate for the body's deterioration. I'm sure it was easier for her, whose immense wealth was almost Nietzschean in its affluent influence and paved the way towards many beneficial connections of *guanxi* in China.

A sudden thought occurred to me that, with whatever I ultimately chose to do with my life, any notion of success that comes with each milestone and personal accomplishment, or sense of reputation that comes with fame, would not amount to anything of notable importance to me; however, if I were to become so filthily and mindlessly rich, that would really be something.

How was that ever going to happen? What is success when everything around you is that big, whereas you are only this small?

It's all a lottery but I felt that I was about to get lucky.

I got dressed and went to wait for Luna on the corner of Hengshan Lu and Wanping Lu.

I resisted the temptation of popping into the many bookstores in the vicinity for fear of being late but couldn't resist picking up some *shengjianbao* on my way over. I'd grown really fond of this pan-fried, pork bun, crispy and tangy with vinegar on the outside, while soft and succulent on the inside. It was unlike anything the Malaysian Chinese—who were largely descendants of southern Chinese migrants—ate back home, and so shengjianbao was always a treat for me, one that I made sure I took my time to savour each and every steamy morsel. As tempting as it was to swallow the baozi whole, you would surely burn your throat doing so, although even then it would be completely worth it.

When I left my apartment, it had looked to be nothing more than a cool day in late summer, but now the sun was lost in an overcast grey sky and I wished that I'd had the foresight to bring an umbrella. I was wearing my blue Oxford shirt with brown corduroy elbow patches. This piece was by an independent menswear brand in Malaysia called Shuren. On the label was a legend which explained through its eponymous proverb that Shuren meant tree-man, literally relating a man's personal growth to be more difficult than that of a tree. What that had to do with clothing I wasn't sure, but I appreciated the detailed cross-stitching over the wide wales of corduroy. Now I was left looking in vain for the sun's re-emergence and felt silly that another one of my favourite shirts might be ruined by the rain.

As I walked on, my cell phone began to vibrate deep inside my pocket, ringing the same humdrum tune every time I pulled it out. It was my mother calling again from Malaysia, although I never felt obliged to answer her calls. Ever since I moved here, she would telephone from time to time only to ask me the same thing, and I had long since grown tired of her constant bellyaching about how I fell short of her expectations.

When are you coming home? Are you seriously going to continue living in China? Malaysia isn't that bad, what? You know so-and-so got married, apparently not because they had an accident in bed. Someone else bought his wife a new car, barely got the loan approved after financing their condo, so I've heard. Someone else bought himself a new wife! Well, I hope the mainlanders aren't being rude to you. Are you eating well at all? I might come over for a visit soon. I'll let you know, okay? OKAY?

But of course, I always answered her calls.

What choice did I have?

'Would it be so hard to answer your phone the first time I call?'

'Forgive me, Mother. My hearing turns selective on the weekend.'

I had never told my mother about Luna and so it was unlikely that she would ever truly understand my reasons for moving to China—although I wasn't exactly sure why I hadn't explained it to her. Perhaps, deep down, I dreaded being at the receiving end of the disapproval of my mother and the rest of my extended family if they were to discover I'd come all the way to China just to be stood up by an online lover. I was simply unwilling to deal with their preconceived notions of a collective shame, which I considered was purely self-inflictive, and something they were very keen to hand over to me as if it were a baton in a relay race.

'You're not still using those dating apps, are you?'

'Not so much any more; but I was only following in your footsteps, Mother.'

My mother laughed. She had always maintained that she went on those Tinder dates as an April Fool's joke.

'Why don't you come home, dear? I'll find you a good wife in no time. Everyone loves a UK graduate.'

'I was in Bath for only three months.'

'They don't know that. Plus, it doesn't discount the fact that you graduated from an English institute.'

'I have to go now. I'm about to meet a friend.'

'Oh lovely. A friend I'll be able to meet soon?'

'Let's not get ahead of ourselves. Today's my first time meeting her.'

'Promise you'll give me a heads up if you're going to marry a communist?'

'I'm going to hang up now.'

'Love you.'

We hung up. In the phone log I scrolled through all the calls I had missed from her, and realized it was almost a year since I last called her. Mother was always the one who initiated contact.

I must've spent a good two hours waiting around Xujiahui Park, but Luna never showed. I didn't text or call her. There really wasn't any need to do so.

I fished out my phone, but the only one who had called me had been my mother.

For the first time in a long time, I opened up the Tinder app, where there were about ten unread messages waiting for me. I had put Tinder notifications on mute when I first made plans to meet Sofia, as that was around the time I switched from translating to writing, and since then, improving my work had consumed vast amounts of my time.

I still couldn't reach Sofia on WeChat, but since spending the night together she had sent me two messages on Tinder. *I had fun the other night, let's meet again sometime if you want to. You like duck blood soup, right?* she had written, and in the second message, she left me her phone number.

I locked my screen, not knowing what to think.

Sofia made me think of cigarettes, and I wanted a smoke.

Switching on my phone again, I proceeded to scroll through the messages from my other Tinder matches.

I wasn't a guy who got a lot of likes or messages on dating apps. It just wasn't me to put up good, well-thought-out pictures with a witty bio to go along with it and so I had simply used some old pictures of myself that I happened to have, taken by my friends who had gotten into photography during our university time in England, with a piece of prose attached to my profile that I'd chanced upon when browsing one of the many Chinese forums, which roughly translated to:

Love dwells far beyond sea and mountain—
Great lie of the land, one cannot flatten

I shall be ferried across ocean by boat
Taking long trail through high mountain post

All standing before me will become appeased
Still unquiet is the heart awaiting release.

I loved the way the poem sounded since the very first time I read it, and I would've readily credited its author if I knew who it was. It spoke to me deeply through the imagery it evoked, and I got the sense that I was in one of those Chinese ink paintings, gliding down a river by the great Jiangshan in a fishing boat, as I trawled my net through its glassy waters. Its simple beauty resonated with me, and each time I conjured up the image in my mind, it was always a profound one, be it with its dark waters rising up to the mountains like a fjord, or my trawling my fishing net through a vast sea.

I sat down on a bench as I scrolled through my messages. It was usually either just a hi or something funny like *wish I could go that deep *wink emoji**.

Right then, I received a new message from a girl called Rei.

'Nike Air Max 1s in Xujiahui Park? Bit old, still handsome,' she wrote in Mandarin.

Instinctively, I looked down at my beaten-up pair of red-and-white Air Max 1s, so soiled and creased beyond recognition that I had almost forgotten what they were called. The second thing I did was to take stock of my surroundings: a couple of aunties power walking and talking, an expat dismounting from his bicycle and flicking a cigarette away, a group of old men engrossed in a game of Chinese chess and some university students conducting what appeared to be an elaborate, bridal photoshoot that looked to involve a presumably very state-of-the-art tech gadget . . .

My first guess was that Rei was one of the university students, texting me out of boredom from a protracted photography session. The sun didn't look like it was due to emerge from the mass of dark clouds any time soon and morning seemed to be getting away from all of us, but yet the students pushed on with their photoshoot, sweating profusely in their tee shirts and jeans, wholly absorbed in angling the round, disc reflectors every which way to cheat the fading light into the camera shutter aimed at the demure bride beneath the veil.

I did a quick head-to-toe of everyone there who seemed to be already packing up, then tapped on Rei's Tinder profile and swiped through her pictures as if for the very first time, as I couldn't recall swiping right on her profile at all. She definitely had a unique style of dressing, not what you would call fashionable in the high-street sense, but always with a sense of style she could call her own. A chemise col Claudine with black slacks and high heels, a librarian tweed blazer with Jean Paul Sartresque glasses, a 1940s Manchurian qipao with subtle phoenix embroidery. In every one of her pictures, she had on a different outfit, and so my eyes flitted from phone to every woman in the park and back. No. She couldn't be one of the students with perspiration seeping through their shirts in dark patches, nor any of the office ladies doing yoga in spandex by the water. She seemed so much more elegant than that, well dressed to the point that you'd instantly recognize if you saw her.

I felt uneasy and decided not to reply just yet and got up from the bench to make a round of the park in search of my mystery texter. Well perhaps she wasn't all that mysterious, as I had access to her Tinder profile right here on my phone. It wrote:

If you let me dress you, one day, I might just undress for you.

Was she a stylist of some sort?

Oh.

Okay.

Now I really needed to find this woman.

I kept my eyes peeled as I walked, more wary than ever of the shoes on my feet. I didn't find her feeding rice to the sparrows by the lake, or watching the wind ripple the still waters from under the willow tree either. In fact, the park, usually a hotspot for couples and weekenders in summer, was all but completely deserted today because of the overcast skies.

I must've made it halfway around the lake before giving up my search. I didn't even bother trying the old memorial chimney to the southwest of the park; I couldn't understand why anybody ever went there anyway. Instead, I climbed the sightseeing bridge overlooking the middle of the park, feeling suddenly like a dog that had forgotten where its bone was buried. As I looked into the distance beyond the park, everything around me began to manifest itself in subtly differentiated tones of grey, from the concrete footpaths cast in shadows, to the shroud of smog reflected in the surface of the lake. I felt as though I owed Shanghai an apology for feeling such malaise.

I felt tired. Tired of doing and feeling nothing all the time. I needed a cigarette, but no longer bothered to carry a pack with me. What was the point. Did I really need any more grey in my life?

I thought about Luna. I thought about how I should process the fact that she hadn't shown up. Like a hot summer's sirocco, she had swept right through me on a whim, leaving me by my lonesome on the streets of Shanghai, awaiting the fall of sycamore leaves in autumn. I likened her to the tiny pockets of heat that came in waves, invisible, oppressive and most unwelcome, although part and parcel of Shanghai's rainy summer cycle.

Since coming here, it had been nice to experience the progression of seasons, something that was non-existent in Malaysia. It allowed me to sense what the changing seasons represented as the greater balance in the grand scheme of things on this earth. Having grown up in a tropical climate, I had always found it difficult to wrap my head around the idea of solstices or the equinox. Equally, explanations about daylight savings confused the hell out of me (they might as well have been talking about the multiverse theory). Are our emotions just as susceptible to change like the seasons are? or do we come to feel particular sentiments according to the time of year? I couldn't answer. At the end of the day, I wasn't one who made a habit of retrieving winter clothing from the storage unit as soon as the temperatures dropped with the falling leaves.

I spent the first winter of my life waiting for the wind, wondering when the bursts of heat would arrive in full force once again. But what I would learn was that however long I waited in eager anticipation, the zephyrs would always catch me off guard, rushing to caress me hard and fast in its pockets of hot currents before dispersing onwards for other lands no sooner than I turned around.

Somehow, I was always left behind in its hot, dry wake.

The northern entrance to Xujiahui Park was a desolate scene by the time evening rolled around.

Having hidden behind the clouds all day, the sun hadn't bothered to show itself for sunset either. The only people left in the park now, apart from a few joggers and myself, were the aunties who had just finished their afternoon session of plaza dancing and were now leisurely packing up their radios and paper fans after an evening spent moving their bodies in poorly attempted synchrony. Some of them would now go home for a well-earned rest, others to hastily scare up a meal for the family, refilling their own bellies as well before hurrying back to the park in time for the nighttime session. I, on the other hand, didn't feel like eating and hadn't felt any appetite for a long time.

I resumed my seat on the steel bench. The university students had finished their photoshoot and were all gone by now, save the model who had since changed out of her quasi-betrothal costume, now in a colour-block, cropped sweatshirt and high-waisted, straight jeans hemmed perfectly to sit on top of a pair of mint Nike trainers. There really was no need for me to scrutinize the face behind the purple-tinted, cat's-eye glasses; from her style I could sense that very same individuality for which I had been scouring the park and instinctively knew that this was Rei standing a few metres from me.

The weekend outfit, which she now sported, gave off a light and easy vibe similar to her style showcased in her Tinder photos. In her presence I couldn't help but feel gauche with my shabby clothing and uncoordinated ensemble. I felt that simply being in the presence of someone so impeccably dressed would do wonders for my ego.

'Well, it took you long enough; were you waiting for the moonlight to guide you over?' Rei said.

I looked up at the moon, now a luminous mass obscured by the smog, seething away like a cyst under the skin—why was I expecting to find something there of all places?

'I was actually looking all over for you. Were you the one wearing a bridal gown earlier?'

'Hmm . . . yes and no. There were two of us modelling just now.'

'Really? I hadn't noticed. I was busy looking for you.'

We exchanged small talk, and very quickly I came to realize that I had judged her rather too hastily by her Tinder dating profile. Somehow, I had presumed she was the type who would pester a guy to take her shopping, who spent hours on end in Xintiandi, browsing the latest offerings in women's fashion, expecting to be pampered. Now she was telling me about style and complaining about the quirky demands their fussy marketing director placed on her team, and very quickly I knew she was far from the princess-syndrome type. I couldn't keep myself from admiring her casual Sunday outfit, and I couldn't help wondering where she had picked up such a fine pair of raw selvedge denim, something you don't see women wear all that much.

So, I asked her where she had gotten them, and whether she would take me there.

Right now? she asked. Yes, right now, I nodded.

'Actually, I was kind of hoping to hang out and talk with you. I was watching you all afternoon. I couldn't help but wonder . . . how does one get their shoes so dirty? We'd better get them cleaned for you, or perhaps even shop for some new ones?'

There I went again, going further down the rabbit hole of online dating, hoping that beyond the swiping, the back and forth flirting and the moments of warmth between two individuals, was something other than a momentary companionship which would eventually dissolve into bitter disappointment. Rei seemed nice and normal enough. She was beautiful and very nice to me. With the midsoles of my Air Maxes subtly cracking beneath my weight, what harm was there in acquiring a new pair of shoes in my life?

That evening, I journeyed with Rei to the very fringes of the French Concession to have my shoes cleaned and when Luna texted me halfway through with the two words *I'm sorry*, I just ignored her and put my phone away.

There were many sneaker stores all over Changle Lu, many of which the editor had mentioned to me to help me in my coverage of streetwear. You can get anything you want: Jordans for retail or resell; Supreme bogos from New York; Palace Trifergs from the UK, you name it. Although I was very surprised to learn from Rei that these daigou brands didn't sell as well as one would think.

'In recent years, Zhongguoren have become very patriotic about the Chinese brands that drive the nation's trends. Ten years ago was a completely different time; people back then were crazy about Japanese fashion and the hip-hop style from the 90s.'

'Nike Dunks were a big thing back then, right? when the whole, skate-boarding movement was going international?'

'I guess so. But not that many people skate here any more. I mean . . . they might have boards, but they don't actually skate. It's all about Yeezies and Off-White lumberjack shirts for their WeChat moments, or Instagram if you're *international* like that.'

'And Tinder?'

'Yes, precisely! Aren't you smart!' she snickered.

My shoes looked much cleaner after the 100-yuan cleaning service, which was basically a glorified wipe down with fragrant and very foamy soap. What the shoe cleaner couldn't do anything about however was the yellowing soles and sheer wear on my Air Maxes. Rei said she liked the vintage look it exuded, that it was kind of *OG* (original gangster) without saying that I was trying too hard—whatever that meant.

I ended up picking up a new pair of white-and-grey Air Max 1s without trying them on first, and Rei had a go at me for not being adventurous enough to try something new. Go ahead, try them on! You'll see that you look like a granddad, she said. I told her I already knew how they would fit, and that I was not a granddad because granddads needed to first have offspring of their own, and I was going to die alone.

Upon leaving the first store, we immediately found ourselves browsing the wares of another. Then another. And another.

Shopping with her felt surreal, with her every movement and deliberation on various articles of clothing so effortless it was like she was operating on the border of unconsciousness. Rei spoke her own language of fashion. She just knew what looked good on a man or a woman, of any age and for any occasion, although it was the fact that I was with her that put me at ease.

By the end of our little shopping spree, she'd bought herself some long, woollen socks and a dainty maroon beret, *for the coming autumn*, she said. I feigned a smile, as I followed behind, hauling her plastic bags of sneakers, raw denim jeans and a stainless-steel bracelet that I already seemed to have misplaced. I felt the entire weight of my purchases cut deep into the palms of my hands, and my pocket.

'Do you feel better now?' she asked me after we picked up two cups of *boba* tea. I could feel the buzz of sugar coursing through my body with every sip.

'I guess so. But what about?'

'Oh, I don't know? You were waiting about in the park for a good few hours; there must have been a lot on your mind.'

'I'm just missing home; I haven't been back for a while now.'

'Hmm . . . where in the south are you from?'

'Well, I'm from a little farther south than the south.'

'Oh. Wait. Are you Vietnamese?!'

'What? No, I'm Malaysian. But good guess.'

'You speak Putonghua so well for a foreigner . . . although you look nothing like a foreigner.'

'Well, ethnically I'm what you would call Han Chinese; you know, there's a large overseas Chinese community in Malaysia.'

'But what about the language? Do they teach Mandarin in schools over there?'

'Only if you choose to enrol in a Chinese school; there are some Chinese people back in Malaysia who don't even know how to write their names in Mandarin. Like they might go eat at a hawker centre, only to ask every hawker what they were selling because they can't read the signage.'

'So . . . do you mean there are other types of schools in Malaysia? In different languages?'

'Pretty much. One gets to choose whether they want to be Chinese or not.'

'Interesting . . . this explains a lot. I have Chinese colleagues who were born overseas, they don't speak more than a couple of phrases in Mandarin, and they hate to be referred to as Zhongguoren.'

'Do they dislike being associated with the nationality or the Chinese race itself?'

'Can't speak for them, but last I checked, Taiwanese isn't a race, Hong Kongese isn't a race, Singaporean isn't a race, and Malai isn't a race! Some of these people . . . it's like they want to live in China and feel what it's like to be Chinese, but just refuse to be called Zhongguoren.'

It's quite simple, I wanted to tell her, the fact is they just don't identify as Zhongguoren. But eventually I went with a different route.

'It's a shame that Zhongguoren now appears to be a divisive term, rather than the original unifying one. But was the term ever unifying if we really think about it?'

'What do you mean? Of course, it's unifying! We're all part of a greater Zhonghua minzu.'

'I guess so,' I said, even though I didn't agree. 'But, you see, at the end of the day, from a global point of view, it doesn't say "People's Republic of China" on the passports of your foreign colleagues either.'

'I guess not. But what's wrong with being Chinese? After all, that's the reason these people chose to move here in the first place, right? To learn about Chinese culture?'

'You can't blame them if they want to have a clear distinction between ethnicity and nationality, right? Like for example,

I'm from Malaysia, but I'm Chinese all the same. And you know what? Malay is an actual race in Malaysia, and we speak Bahasa Malaysia as our national language.'

'Oh, does that make you a Malay?'

I laughed . . . in my mind I consigned whoever invented nationalism to eternal damnation. The idea of race too, insofar as the idea presupposes and indicates there to be one entirely homogenous kind of people across post-colonial nations with multiple ethnic groups was a flawed and doomed concept.

'In the context of our conversation, I guess I'm Malay, yes. On the outside, though, I'm as yellow as SpongeBob SquarePants.'

She almost burst out laughing and raised one hand to hold down a mouthful of boba pearls.

'That sponge baby? I love him so much!'

I smiled. She was cute when she snorted boba.

'So why did you want to come to China . . . isn't it much more pleasant in Malaysia? I've only heard good things about life in the Nanyang, with the long, sandy beaches, pristine island resorts and smelly, fragrant durian.'

I finished my tea and disposed of the cup in a bin nearby. I had hardly touched the pearls—so full of starch.

'I came to China to meet this girl, my ex-girlfriend to be exact.'

'Hmm . . .' she paused and bit the straw. 'It's like whenever I've pigeon-holed you, you just jump right out of it!'

'Well, this is the thing.'

'What is it, Mr A-Little-Farther-South-Than-South? Did you come here to win back her love?'

'I'd like to, but there's a slight problem.'

'Oh, don't tell me, you found out that she's already married?'

'If only it were that simple.'

'Then what?'

'We fell in love on the Internet. I've never met the woman in my life.'

Chapter 9

During my days as a young man only just discovering his virility, I had always dreamed of sleeping with a lot of women.

This particular folly of my youth was far from any Dionysian yearning nor one driven by carnal desire or the primal for genetic propagation. Rather it was a fantasy driven by the wide array of smartphone pornography circulated among classmates in the conservative, all-boys government school I went to. Porn was illegal and forbidden, and that is why it felt like emancipation, and something much more than a juvenile curiosity to all of us at school, who were not nearly precocious enough to know about the male gaze, or what to expect at all during sex.

When sex was eventually expected of me, I had always assumed that I would become aroused and be able to perform on cue regardless of how drunk, tired or nervous I was—although these were never factors that I expected to be problematic in the first place. It would only become clear to me in the coming years that sexual arousal was not a thing that came easy for me, and that my desire would become relegated to the role of advisor from that of instigator.

My problems with sexual desire only seemed to worsen when I came to China. It was around the time when Luna started to avoid every method of contact that I initiated with her. My messages were left un-replied, calls were missed and she even unfollowed me on social media a handful of times only to follow back sometime later. I don't mean to suggest that the two phenomena were directly correlated, only that their coinciding with each other left me feeling as though I had incurred some form of karmic punishment which had accumulated beyond its limit and was now being duly meted out to me.

I hadn't replied to Luna's apology sent on the day of our failed meeting, and I didn't plan to. After close to a year's build-up in anticipation of our meeting, where many a day was spent brooding in agony, angst and anxiety as to the when and whether we would actually meet, I now felt oddly at ease with the idea of never speaking to her again, and so that was the line of thought I chose to implement.

As soon as I had actually taken a moment to lay bare the timeline of events that had occurred between us—from our getting together online which, although absurd, felt so right in the moment; to our abrupt breakup for reasons that remained a mystery to me and her subsequent reaching out for emotional support whenever it was convenient; to her reneging on her promise of meeting me in person if I happened to come to China on my travels—it became easier to come to terms with the way the events had played out.

I had to swallow the hard but simple truth that she meant more to me than I did to her.

A few weeks after our failed rendezvous at Xujiahui Park, I found myself overwhelmed with a very bad case of writer's block, which in my relatively short three months of working full-time as a writer, had never happened before.

After turning in what I felt to be a series of mediocre articles covering topics on the art of travelling alone, minimalistic living in Shanghai and the best skin-care brands for working adults, the editor summoned me to her office one day and told me that my next story was to be on ShanghaiPRIDE.

'I have to say I know absolutely nothing about it, save the fact that it's a LGBTQIA event,' I told her, not wanting to disappoint in case I turned in a piece of work that would let down the entire LGBT community.

'I'll give you a piece of advice,' she said, holding up the unlit cigarette towards my face, 'It doesn't matter how good or bad a writer you are, one should never make excuses before approaching a piece of writing. You hear me?'

I nodded. She was right, I was making lame excuses for myself. There was no reason I couldn't write this piece.

'Don't worry. Most people don't even know the festival exists, even though this year's event will mark a decade since ShanghaiPRIDE's inception. Having said that, keep in mind that the ten-year anniversary is a big thing for the LGBT community, and since Chinese coverage of the event is highly censored, it's up to the foreign media to provide a fair coverage of the festival in its full authenticity.'

The editor lit her cigarette, and I waited for her to go on, but that was it.

'It's quite a big topic,' I said.

She took a drag, the fumes in the unventilated room felt suffocating.

'You wouldn't happen to be homophobic?'

'No,' I said after thinking about it for a while. 'I don't really have an opinion about it one way or another.'

'Well then, we don't have a problem. I'm a little homophobic myself, not that I don't have a ton of gay friends in the city; it's just that I wouldn't know what to do if my daughter told me she was gay, but that's what they call "heteronormativity" in English, the lens through which a straight person views the world. Heteronormative does not mean cisgender though, so don't get it confused.'

Sis-gender? I should write that down. Wait. A daughter? That was news. He-te-ro-nor-ma-ti-vi-ty? I couldn't even pronounce half of it.

'You'll be fine. Listen, there's always room for improvement for every writer but, at the moment, that's not something you should be overly concerned with. I've read every one of your articles to date; what you need to find is your niche and a form to present it in. In the meantime . . . just enjoy the ride.'

Another drag, another sigh of smoke.

I began my research on ShanghaiPRIDE later that afternoon, and quickly read up on the history and evolution of the event through the years, of how it transitioned from a small cultural celebration in the year of its inception to the full-fledged parade it was today.

Browsing through the pictures on the festival's official website and social-media pages, I was confronted with the existence of a queer world that I had only been vaguely aware of for the greater part of my life.

Heteronormativity—was that what the editor had said in English? I looked that up too but struggled to find its Mandarin equivalent.

Admittedly, I had no idea how to approach the writing of this article. The topic itself felt so entirely far away from me, and at the same time, it wasn't something I could simply approach objectively from an outsider's angle. It was a position I wasn't used to being in as a writer.

Half in frustration and half out of lack of something to do, I got up from my work desk for a cup of the insipid filter coffee everyone at the office loathed. But perhaps they only loathed it in theory because, although there were much better artisanal cafés to cater to the zombie-mob of writers and designers in the area, this filter coffee practically tasted like the petrol that fuelled us. It gave everyone a working-class feel for struggle if they wanted it.

The machine was situated at the rear corner of the pantry, all the way down the corridor of asbestos partitions, the walls plastered with numerous awards and notable news articles by

TRIESTE, which served the purpose of reminding one more of work in the short time spent walking away from it.

The machine was so slow that, whenever an intern or anyone new joined the team, we liked to send them to the pantry to get us coffee, all in the name of character building of course. This was something of a rite of passage that even we went through when we joined; a frustrating wait for the dripping of coffee that would often spew and splutter without warning. What we would do was send interns in by themselves, and then have people whom they didn't know go form a large queue waiting for coffee. Those in queue would cuss and shout while smoking cigarettes, and by the time the interns finally realized what was happening, we would already be having an impromptu break that felt like a party.

But the pantry was empty this afternoon, devoid of the usual waxed-haired douchebags hitting on the interns and the gossiping office ladies eager to recap their weekends. I savoured the peaceful moment, taking in the onset of fall through the water-stained windows, as the whir of the coffee machine droned on behind me.

Then the dripping stopped, and my coffee was ready.

Quiet. I hadn't felt it in a while.

After my coffee, I suddenly found myself craving Malaysian food, so I delayed the writing of my article in search of some *nasi lemak* in Shanghai.

I took the short bus ride north towards Jing'an to a restaurant run by a Chinese auntie from Penang. The food there was excellent but, of course, didn't compare to the greasy fills you would get back home, and I always enjoyed coming here when I was sick of the canteen food and the monotony of Waimai. Sometimes I could score a bigger portion simply by sweet talking the young Malaysian part-timers who had come to Shanghai for university, but the auntie caught on to my coquetry very quickly, and before

I knew it, the students were calling me 'big uncle', or 'the guy who looks more youthful than he actually is'.

After lunch, I found myself repeatedly and automatically reaching for my phone and then clicking the screen on and off in disgust before returning it to my pocket.

Lethargic, slow, uninspiring. That was how the last few weeks had been for me. Without a doubt this reflected in my work, and with the unforgiving state of the blogosphere these days where people scrolled through text faster no sooner than they could digest its title, no writer was safe from the wrath of the commenters who merely skim-read the pieces and judged them solely based on the images and their captions rather than the context of the whole thing. I did, of course, have my fair share of loyal readers who tended to respond positively in the comments but, seeing as I was still relatively new to the scene, I couldn't afford to risk losing any of them with more of the same form of anecdotes I had been churning out of late.

Something had to change and it had to change quickly.

My phone vibrated on silent in my pocket, but I had to get my move on. With every few steps a new unread entered my inbox, and with every gob of saliva I spat out, I felt the urge to hurl the damned thing on to the gravel.

Did I have to post a picture of my nasi lemak on Instagram? I had consciously made my phone ingest the meal before me, and in that allowed it to provoke a greater hunger in the realm of the Internet, unconsciously propagating a chain of desire for the spicy and savoury dish. What the picture didn't convey was how obscenely sweet the sambal tasted when it was supposed to be spicy, or how the soul of the dish, in its coconut rice, was bland and overly large in its quantity. I would've loved the people who commented on how delicious it looked to go to Malaysia for an authentic pack of coconut rice wrapped in banana leaf.

The vibration of messages gradually slowed before ceasing altogether. The obvious question for me then was, had Luna texted? How was I supposed to know, when I had already blocked her on every messaging app?

In every great love story, there tend to be themes of separation between two lovers, of great ordeals to be overcome, be it in the form of class, political or religious differences, in order to be together.

Could I be separated from someone who didn't want to see me?

Was I in love with Luna?

I felt like a fool for asking these questions. How could I have been so serious about an online relationship in the first place?

What the hell was all of this then?

How could my feelings feel so real?

I only attended to my phone when I was back at my apartment that night, where I spent a good amount of time scrolling through the pages of unread notifications, *not smoking a cigarette.*

It took me a while to go through the sea of comments, every one of which I read, while complying with the meaningless cordialities of exchanging likes that people took way too seriously.

The process was gruelling. From what I had learnt after years of being on social media, it mattered not whether you tagged a restaurant's location with the intent for all to see, someone dumb enough was bound to comment *WHERE IS THIS*, effectively negating any notion of Darwinian evolution. Then, there were the emojis—don't even get me started on those.

A peculiar notification in my inbox made me break from scrolling through the comments. Buried in my Instagram message requests was a user I had never seen before, who, in replying to my post, had sent a series of pictures of nasi lemak and teh tarik that looked so authentic they were presumably taken at Malaysian mamak stalls.

The account was private, with no pictures and a few bot-account followers to its name. With a jumble of numbers for a username, I had no idea who this was or why the pictures were sent.

My first guess was that some idiot friend of mine back home had accidentally sent me these pictures from his *xiaohao,* an alternative account one would use to stealthily flirt with people you're not supposed to. He had probably found it funny to see people raving about a third-rate serving of nasi lemak, that he sent me many pictures of food from home to make me jealous. Or said person might have gotten so drunk that he had me confused with another person altogether and took me for one of the many women he had gotten to know at the KTV lounges or *Diaohua chang.*

I decided to greet the anonymous sender with a LOL, hoping to gauge from his or her response who might be behind the pictures with flashes so bright it made the mamak stall look like a nightclub.

A reply came instantly.

Guess where I am, the message from sappho31 read.

It could just as well have been any username, but seeing those words left me in no doubt as to who it was.

Luna. She had always said she wanted to visit Malaysia again. What was she doing there now? Another family trip perhaps?

Just thinking about her made me feel uneasy, causing me to fluctuate between an emotional state of elation and despair. Why did I always have to get so upset about her? It had taken me long enough to come to terms with the fact that I was in love with a woman I had never met. Drawn out and protracted had been the road to my acceptance that, in all likelihood, I would never see her face to face in this lifetime. Her hold on me was so strong, that I didn't even care to know for certain if this was her texting me. A simple text was all it took to bury my ills.

I'll fly back to see you, I typed out, then immediately deleted it.

I flicked the lock screen on my phone on and off again, wanted a smoke real bad, wondered if I could tolerate its foul goodness again. The permutations of possibilities crept into my head but left before I could actually ponder and act on them.

Desire was something that I had struggled to muster throughout the entire Shanghai summer, and now that fall was here, I all but felt that that sense of yearning was about to abandon me for good.

Was there something I had to do in order to rediscover my virility? or did this have to do with a more pressing matter, that deep down, I was really that lonely a person?

sappho31 told me she was visiting the islands of Semporna, where it was so isolated that it provided the world's best spots for snorkelling and scuba diving.

'You don't know how to scuba dive.'

'I want to learn. You know, I've changed my hair colour to ultramarine so it matches the sea here.'

'You and your chameleon hair.'

'Maybe that's what I want to be—a beautiful, shape-shifting rainbow chameleon. In fact, I'm thinking of getting a tattoo here.'

'But a chameleon can't change a tattoo once it's inked.'

'Be supportive. Give me some suggestions!'

'How about the moon in that Van Gogh painting . . .?'

'The waning crescent moon in *The Starry Night*?'

'Uh huh.'

'Apparently astronomical records show it was a waning gibbous moon at the time when Van Gogh painted *The Starry Night*. I like the moon in *A Walk at Twilight* better . . . but no.'

'Either would suit you well.'

For a long time after that she didn't reply. In the eagerness of talking to her, I had missed the chance to ascertain how she felt about me. But how was I even supposed to ask that?

'Who are you with over there?' I finally wrote.

'A very beautiful woman whom I love.'

I didn't quite know what to make of that.

'My mother just told me she wants to visit China in a couple of months,' I wrote.

'Oh, really? My mother isn't talking to me, it's like I'll be disowned soon.'

'What's wrong?'

'She didn't want me travelling alone with a woman.'

'Is it cause it's dangerous?'

'Let's talk about your mom instead. It'll almost be winter when she comes. Is this a bid to haul the prodigal son home?' she asked, exhaling heavily via voice note, sounding as though she couldn't wait to blow out the cigarette smoke before she spoke.

'My mother . . . she wants to do one of those *xungen* things.'

'Really? Oh wow! I thought only people from China did that. And where is *laojia* for your family?'

Both my mother and I considered Malaysia to be home, so I thought I'd tell her where our ancestors were from instead.

'Guangdong for Mother, but it seems like she wants to visit the place from where my ancestors originated.'

'And which province would that be?'

'That . . . I'll have to ask when I see her.'

'Yeah, I'm interested to know too. You Malaysians are so interesting.'

'Luna, don't you ever want to meet me?'

And then she disappeared from my life again.

Chapter 10

The days merged into one another as I wrote. My mother was due to arrive in Shanghai from Kuala Lumpur in less than two weeks.

I was tasked with buying us both plane tickets to Sanya in Hainan province, which had since developed something of a price premium with the cold setting in around the country. Sanya, of course, was the southernmost province of China off from the mainland, with its own tropical-monsoon climate that made it a prime tourist destination throughout the year. Even during the colder winter months, Sanya's averaged a pleasantly welcoming temperature of 20°C which, based on reviews from the forums, was apparently perfect weather for the beach.

On any given day in Malaysia, it was the ideal temperature for a thunderstorm.

'Oh God. What have you been eating? So thin!'

'I've actually gained 5 kg, Ma,' I said, hugging her before carrying her bags outside through the arrival gates.

'Feels like 5 kilos of bone to me! Let's go get some food, la. Finally, I get to try some authentic mala hot pot!'

'That's Sichuanese food, Mother. We'll have to go all the way westward to Sichuan for that. How about some *xiaolongbao* or pork belly herbal soup?'

'Wow . . . did I raise a fascist? Any mala hot pot here would be better than that diluted filth they serve you in Malaysia. Your mother wants hot pot, darling. And when you're free, why don't you order me a few packs of the real paste from Chongqing to bring home?'

'But we're leaving in a couple of days, I'm not sure if the Chinese couriers are that efficient.'

'Well, send it to the hotel in Sanya then! Taobao, no? Come, Mommy's hungry now. Don't worry, la! We'll order the *yinyang* pot so you can take the clear broth and leave the good spicy stuff to me.'

It didn't take long for Mother to settle in and get going in China.

I loved her, but most of the time she was so difficult to be around. This wasn't your typical Asian mother who disapproved of anything her son did that wasn't good enough for her. On the contrary, it was frustrating for me because she gave no opinion on matters when I needed her opinion the most, and I felt that she saw no point that I ever did anything at all.

But could I really blame her for my decisions?

I had never explained my reasons in full for moving to China to Mother. Not why I chose the city of Shanghai, nor why I was working as a content writer when I could be pursuing a more stable career back home in Malaysia where, even though there was more to be demanded in terms of salary and economic growth, the relative standard of living was arguably better than China; where things were more affordable and you didn't have to win the lottery to buy a house.

My mother never questioned or asked me about what I did in my life, and that was the way I wished to keep things—passed over in silence as Ludwig Wittgenstein would say.

There were, of course, times in my life when I had needed the guidance, but felt that Mother always remained insouciant about whatever I brought up, completely oblivious to how important her approval was to me. There was the matter of what to study as a major, which she brought up just the one time with her friends at the Mahjong table over a symphony of clacking tiles. I couldn't bear to stay in the same room with Mother's auntie friends, who were not unlike a wake of vultures who scavenged on fresh gossip and rumours instead of carcasses. It was her opinion I needed, not Auntie Ng or Auntie Lilian's Taoist methods of counsel. But Mother would listen and laugh, only joining in to make appropriate comments that were never particularly snide nor ingratiating, but sufficient to stoke the fire of the conversation.

Throughout my years of growing up, she never spoke of any expectations she had of me or herself for that matter. If I didn't know any better, I would've thought her as extremely unambitious and that she didn't care that much for me at all. But Mother had grown up in a vastly different time, of post-war hardship in a land on the brink of creating its own history, where the Malayan people were eager to prove to the world that they could fare just as well without their British colonizers. Back then, when the line between colonial and free subject was still blurry, marriages continued to form out of the necessity of getting by, and people partook in the institution of matrimony even if it meant that days of economic hardship would only become a little bit more bearable.

For a long time in post-colonial Malaysia, capitalism and the free market had its say in matters of wedlock. Willingly or unwillingly betrothals had to take place, whether arranged by birth or by being deemed suitable enough by the matchmaking *mei po*. Today, the people are able to marry for love or, at the very least, in the name of it. Whether this makes us freer than my mother I cannot say for sure. Because to marry someone in the name of love, is arguably one of the most sublime capitalist ideas the world has ever seen.

There wasn't too much to pack for Sanya.

With the region's year-long summery weather, I could practically dress as I would back home in equatorial Malaysia.

Into my trusty 30L backpack I threw in some khaki shorts and tee shirts, along with enough socks and underwear to last me a few days. I didn't have any sandals or boat shoes for the beach, and so I gave my bathroom slippers a wipe down and wrapped them in plastic. For my shoes I planned to wear that new pair of grey-and-white Air Maxes I had picked up with Rei, the girl from Tinder whom I'd run into at Xujiahui Park. Maybe I could ask her out for a cup of coffee when I got back from Sanya.

But the editor wasn't too pleased at my asking for a whole week off to go holidaying.

'This isn't standard protocol in China. People don't just ask for time off on short notice to fly to Sanya with their mother,' she said, biting a cigarette as usual.

'It's quite important that I do. My mother has been planning this trip for a month.'

'And you only waited until the week before to tell me? I swear, you Southeast Asians . . .'

'. . . we're something else, aren't we?'

'If you know it and I know it, there's really no need to discuss it further. Tell me, will you be able to write there? I'm still expecting that piece on ShanghaiPRIDE from you.'

'About writing there . . . I'm not really sure. Mother wants to do this whole xungen thing, she seems to have already planned an entire week of us touring around the island. The PRIDE piece is almost done, I just have to tune it up a little . . . to not let it seem that heteronormative, as you said before,' I told her, even though the article was nowhere near complete.

'Waaa eii, hold on,' she said, getting very excited. I had a hunch she had thought of a new story for me.

'You never told me that Malaysians cared about their roots in China? I asked you before if you spoke any dialects and you said no!'

'Well, I don't,' I lied, 'but my ma is making it a point to get me reacquainted with my roots.'

'Your roots?'

'My roots.'

'Let's slow down and take a step back,' she said, on her second cigarette now.

'Is your father Zhongguoren?'

'I would think so. Back in the day, nobody outrightly denied being Zhongguoren, even if they were born in the Nanyang. This was way before the whole political identity of "Overseas Chinese" came into being.'

'I'm not sure I understand. But you say you're going to Sanya, so that makes your family Hainanese?'

'Affirmative, the very first Chinese chefs and cooks of Malaya.'

'Were they all Han?'

'No idea. They could have been Han, Mongols or Manchurians for all I know.'

'Fascinating! A boy is forced on a xungen trip to discover his roots when he actually couldn't care less about it! How could you keep this from me all this time?' she exclaimed, now administering herself a third stick of nicotine.

It was obvious what was coming next, the precise reason why I hadn't told her any of this.

'Take your time with the LGBT story, and also the week off for the trip. In return, you'll be writing about your xungen experience on Hainan Island instead.'

There wasn't much I could say to that, what was the point? At the end of the day, the average mainlander would think that all Malaysians were by default ethnically Malay anyway.

'So, can I bum a cigarette?' Mother asked me just as I was scrolling through nothing on my phone.

We were waiting to board at the gate, each holding an americano in hand. Mother almost always only drank kopi-o, except when she couldn't get hold of a cup, then the long black was her go to, claiming it was basically the same thing.

She really took me by surprise. I had no idea she knew and was at a loss about what to say.

'I don't have any, I stopped a few months ago.'

'Is that so? You wouldn't mind if I smoked one though?' she asked, and I watched her pull out a pack with a beach and slanted coconut tree on it. Those did not look good, but she offered me one and I took it very awkwardly. A mother giving her child nicotine! Why did she have a pack anyway? I took one drag and left it at that. It was awful.

We stood in silence. It was only one cigarette, but it felt like an eternity, smoking with your mother. Eventually she laughed, and I laughed.

'Not to your fancy, I take it.'

'Not particularly. What is that dry, earthy taste?'

'It's supposed to be roasted coconut; it says, fragrant and elegant.'

'That's China marketing at its finest.'

'Now don't say that. How would you have described it?'

'How about: *rich in flavour, like freshly microwaved pieces of lead?*' I replied, sipping my coffee. I knew it wasn't good, but humour was never my forte.

'Why do you have cigarettes anyway?' I asked, feeling I had to choose my words carefully.

Mother just laughed. 'We're on holiday, aren't we?' she said.

A fine mist coated Sanya as our plane hovered over the undulating, green landscape. As we descended into the fog for landing, the mist turned into a fine drizzle, which, by the time we got through customs and booked a Didi, was already beginning to clear. I could tell right away that the air was different from Shanghai's, in that it was more humid but crisp with the cool of autumn. On the way to the hotel, I admired the enchanting sight of a clear evening sky as the sun set over kilometres and kilometres of palm oil and coconut estates. It felt just like home, except we were driving down the wrong side of the road.

Mother had booked us a room at The Great Palm of Sanya, one of the many resorts littered around the island. Tucked away in an idyllic corner up a hillock, just off Sanyawan, the low-density resort boasted a mix of villa suites and chalet-style rooms. The one chalet we checked into had awfully high-vaulted, wood ceilings, which gave an illusion of spaciousness in the room for two, even though it wasn't that small to begin with. The en suite bathroom was furnished beautifully with a polished concrete shower and bathtub, replete with all the amenities one could possibly need. The smooth concrete walls extended through into the bedroom, where two queen beds pointed towards a jacuzzi separated by retractable wooden blinds. Beyond that, was a sliding door that led down to the communal barbecue area and swimming pool in the shape of a palm leaf, where the light from the western sunset was now being reflected in the mesmerizingly still waters,

'Did you secretly strike the Toto 4D jackpot, Ma? This room must have cost a bomb . . . I thought we were here on a xungen trip.'

'Don't be impatient, we'll get to that in good time. Let your mother relax for a change.'

'We're in China, people don't understand the concept of relaxing.'

'We're in Sanya, dear. China's very own slow-paced, Southeast Asia. Try to loosen up a bit.'

'I guess I could grab a coffee at the resort café and do some writing on my laptop . . . There's this new piece that the editor has just assigned me.'

'Yes, I'd do that if I were you, without the laptop and work that is. Have you forgotten how to be Malaysian? Just kick back and relax, stop thinking so *Cina* all the time,' mother said.

Cina was a word my mother and I would throw around at times when we felt we were acting too Chinese, or in other words, too highly strung for the wrong reasons. Cina was the Malay word for Chinese, typically to signify people of Chinese race in Malaysia, although in recent times people tended to use it more in the context of referring to mainlanders, while locals of Chinese descent would just identify as Malaysian citizens.

There are, of course, a great number of older Malaysian Chinese folk who are very proud of their Chinese heritage. These are the people who would have no qualms about referring to themselves as Zhongguoren, even if the equivalence of the term meant identifying as a Chinese national. This phenomenon was not so uncommon back in the day throughout the 19th and the 20th centuries, when the Chinese diaspora had moved south, towards the Nanyang, in search of a better life. The Zhongguoren of the Nanyang hailed mostly from the southern provinces of Fujian, Guangdong and Hainan. These Nanyang Chinese were hardy folk, many of whom had journeyed over thousands of kilometres across the ocean to flee from the civil war and the rise of communism in China. Deprived of jobs and opportunities in their impoverished homeland, the Chinese settlers arrived with nothing but dreams of work and wages on Commonwealth soil, and there were few who dared call themselves Zhongguoren if they weren't prepared to break their backs, eking out a living.

I had never given the matter of being Chinese a second thought. For me there existed no confusion between Chinese ethnicity and nationality, no blurred lines between the variegated global Chinese population from the Zhongguoren of China. Nationalism was simply the name of the game in the early 21st century and the primary source of this confusion surrounding identity. After the failures of imperialism and fascism in the past century, world politics is now turning to a different form of exerting power that appears less aggressive. This new form of power is nationalism, where a single nation state and identity are emphasized, trying to bring people together under one unified national identity. At nationalism's most extreme manifestations, we are able to witness events like the Brexit vote and Neo-neoliberal Trumpism in the West, Xinjiang re-education camps and the re-militarization of Japan here in the East, also not forgetting the Israel–Gaza conflict—although I don't even want to talk about all of them, so I'm sorry I brought them up. I looked forward to the demise of nationalism and this manifestation of conservatism but fell short of the foolishness in hoping that it would be at its end anytime soon.

But the concept of a nation wasn't all that bad in itself, was it? Following civil wars throughout history, countries with delineated borders have been formed that are integral to the governance of a nation with functioning economic and immigration policies, complete with their own currency and perhaps most importantly, afforded rights to the citizens that lived there. Nationalism also made possible international sporting events like the Olympics and the World Cup, the highest-level competition imaginable on a world stage, albeit with the capitalism of tourism behind the 'for the good of sports' moniker. Inter-cultural exchange was greatly facilitated with the creation of passports and immigration, allowing people the right of travelling or working in countries foreign to their own.

The real question was whether all this could subsist, or even exist without the formation of nations?

By the time I finished typing up all that I had written in my notebook into the word processor, it was completely dark outside the café.

As I gazed at the residue of the black coffee at the bottom of my cup, doubt began to fester at the back of my mind. I realized that even though I'd made the switch from translating to writing, the work I produced was still in essence, toilet-seat literature. The target audience was still the same social-media users in China who read English. My readers were either foreigners who wanted a peek into daily life and happenings around China, who couldn't afford to be picky with my articles as there weren't that many English writers in the scene to begin with; or Chinese students who wanted to practise and increase their proficiency in reading English.

Was anything I had ever written any good at all? All that I had just written, all that rambling on about identity and nationalism, what was that all about? My goal was to draft up something that could be used in the xungen article which the editor had assigned to me. But wasn't it a tad personal, and not empirical or factual enough? Did every piece of post-colonial writing have to be as comprehensive as a Benedict Anderson text?

It was already past 9 p.m. when Mother finally returned to the hotel room. Not wanting to wait until tomorrow to go swimming, she had left me with my writing at the café to go and check out the palm leaf-shaped pool before it closed for the night. After a long day's travelling and then spending the evening swimming and writing respectively, we were both utterly famished, but far too tired to head downtown for food.

'You go ahead,' my mother said after her shower, 'I don't really want to eat anything at this hour. I might lose sleep if my tummy doesn't digest the food in time.'

'Well, you could've told me earlier, then I wouldn't have waited for you.'

'I'm sorry, dear. The sauna here overlooks the horizon so I stayed a little longer past sunset.'

'A text would've been nice, but you never bring your phone anywhere.'

'Ah boy, you're old enough to make your own decisions, aren't you?'

'Yeah, you're right. I won't wait up next time,' I said, reaching for my phone.

Neither of us spoke for a while. It was really quiet outside.

'All right. I've made my choice,' I said, after choosing a restaurant on the app.

'Oh, did you find a restaurant nearby?'

'Nope. But I'm having food sent via Waimai.'

'Waimai huh . . . what are you getting?'

'Hot pot.'

'Ah . . . hot pot.'

'Want me to order something for you?'

'No . . .'

'You sure, Ma?'

'No . . .'

Mother had never tried any kind of Waimai in China before, let alone the ornate brand of hot pot Waimai that I had just ordered and was now on its way here. The times were quite different back when she used to travel here in the early 2000s. When it was time to eat, her tour group was always put at the mercy of the local guide, and they always ended up eating at some mediocre restaurant in some way affiliated with the tour company, where the food served was typically oily, unsanitary and too heavily seasoned for a Malaysian's palate. There was also the off-putting notion of sharing common dishes with strangers from the same tour group, who had no reservations about sticking their chopsticks into their mouths and back into the dishes over and over again.

'Did you order duck blood?'

She and her duck blood again.

'No, Ma, you didn't tell me you wanted duck blood.'

'But you know that's my favourite, son. How about some cow tongue? Did you get the extra mala soup?'

'First you say you don't want anything, then you say you'll just have a little bit of whatever I order. I can't read your mind, Ma.'

'Aren't those the *must-order* ingredients for a proper hot pot? I expected you to do it right, son.'

I sighed. Already this felt like way too long a trip with Ma.

'Do you want me to call them again and order the duck blood and cow tongue?'

'No, that's fine, dear. You got the half-and-half pot, right? What do they call that again . . .?'

'The yinyang pot?'

'Yes, exactly! As long as there's mala soup!'

'Of course, there's mala soup. There would be little point to mala hot pot if we didn't have the mala soup. I only got the mild-spicy soup though.'

'Oh well . . . that'll have to do.'

For someone who hadn't initially wanted to eat, Mother was quite ecstatic when the food arrived. She gasped in awe as I opened the cardboard box and extracted packages of clear-and-spicy, hot-pot paste, black fungi, an assortment of pork and pork belly, seaweed, lotus root, fragrant mushrooms, coriander, egg dumplings, potato slices, fishballs, dried tofu, regular tofu, peanut and spicy sauce and finally a small yinyang pot made of steel.

'Wow, is that an ACTUAL yinyang pot?' she exclaimed as I tore open the two packages of paste, which I then mixed with water and set over the mini candle stove.

'How fascinating! Oh, and they come with candles as a stove too? Are the flames strong enough to actually cook the food? Do we have to return the pot after our meal?'

'Yup. No, Ma . . . I think you're supposed to keep the pot for future orders. Let's go ahead and eat, shall we? Come help me put the ingredients in.'

'Wait, wait, the soup isn't even hot yet. Let me take a picture with all the ingredients laid out beside the pot first, you know, for Instagram.'

'You need a VPN proxy connection for that; just take a picture with your camera first and I'll help you with the VPN app download later. I'm starving!'

'I already have VPN installed, son. Just hold on to your chopsticks, it'll only take me ten seconds.'

Mother really surprised me at times like this with her presence of mind to download the app in Malaysia, because it was less straightforward to do so after entering the great Chinese firewall of censorship. I watched her hover her phone over the hot pot and its array of plastic-boxed ingredients and waited for the last clicks of the digital shutter to stop.

The broth bubbled steadily beneath the transparent lid, where condensation began to form above the sea of red and white, dichotomized by an S down the middle.

I couldn't wait any longer.

Chapter 11

Mother and I split our time in Sanya between lazing by the beach and relaxing at the resort. When we wanted to eat, we strolled down the boulevard that stretched across from the seaside, to eat at the restaurants offering everything from local fares to the more popular foreign cuisines. When we wanted a drink, there were plenty of pubs and cafés in the area as well. I usually left Mother to herself after lunch, when she liked to have a piña colada or two, while I went off to write at a café thronging with students and couples on holiday. When we reconvened for dinner, Mother always asked how on earth I managed to focus with the constant flux of noisy tourists around me. I told her the endless noise didn't bother me all that much because I wrote best when I was left by myself.

After spending three nights at the Great Palm of Sanya we were ready to leave for our next destination. I had long since given up asking Mother where we were going. She was steadfast in her silence, and frankly I didn't care all that much where we went as long as I got back to Shanghai by next Monday. When we were checking out, she had the hotel concierge hire a local tour van to come pick us up, and from there we would be driven for about an hour to Betelnut Valley, which was Sanya's cultural heritage park famous for its Li and Miao villages.

Just before we departed, I noticed that Mother had a box strapped atop her wheeled suitcase.

'What's this, Ma? A little souvenir for home?'

'Well . . . sort of. It's our yinyang hot pot from the first night,
I didn't want to leave it behind here and let it go to waste.'

I had completely forgotten about the pot but couldn't say that
her wanting to keep it was totally unexpected.

'Mother,' I began, 'why don't you just leave the pot here? I'll
call the hot-pot restaurant to come by and pick it up.'

'But the restaurant gave us the pot for keeps, right?'

'They did. But then we'll be driving round the whole island
with a yinyang pot we don't really need.'

'That's fine, dear. The pot will go right in the boot, and the
driver will be doing all the driving anyway. Look! Here comes our
ride right now!'

The van arrived and pulled up in front of us. I felt helpless as
I watched the driver load our bags along with the yinyang pot into
the van. There wasn't any point in arguing with her now.

The driver did most of the talking during the drive. We didn't
catch his full name, only that his surname was Wang, the most
common surname in China and on earth. We called him Wang
Shifu or Master Wang as a show of respect, and for that he
decided to reward us with a short history lesson.

Wang Shifu explained that Hainan Island was administered by
the Guangdong province up until 1988, and thereafter the island
officially became the country's southernmost province and the
largest special economic zone under Deng Xiaoping's economic
reform. Centuries before all of that happened, from historical
records we know that the first Han Chinese to have come to
Hainan Island was during the Han dynasty around 110 BC, with the
purpose of establishing a military garrison. But as for the Wang
clan, the first pioneer on Hainan Island was Wang Lingong, who,
according to our driver, Wang Shifu, had most certainly come from
the Wang clan in Nanjing, and following the birth of his three sons,
had marked the inception of the Wang clan on Hainan Island.

I was only half-listening to Wang Shifu's tour-guide trivia and I could tell my mother didn't really know how to respond to him. In fact, I wasn't that keen on revealing that we were from Malaysia, as being a foreign tourist made one an easy target for guides to milk you dry, usually by making unneeded stops at local-produce shops or by forcing you to dine at restaurants that were all part of an elaborate tourism syndicate.

But then my mother went and told Wang Shifu that it was so interesting he had said that because discovering our roots was precisely the reason we were here, as a mother-and-son duo from Malaysia travelling Hainan on a long overdue xungen trip.

I guess that was that.

'You speak Putonghua really well! Are you Zhongguoren from Malaysia?' the driver asked.

'My son and I are both Mandarin-educated. I made it a point for him to go to a Chinese school.'

'Oh, wow! Zhongguoren are really so talented everywhere around the world. I hear that we Zhongguoren control the economy in Malaysia, right? No matter where fate places us on this earth, even in the harshest of hardships and cruellest of climates, we'll survive.'

Kind of like cockroaches, I felt like saying.

'Earlier when the hotel told me you were from Malaysia, I thought they meant that you were ethnic Malay people!'

Hadn't he just praised, only moments ago, the Malaysian Chinese people for doing so well for themselves over the years? Why was it always so hard for people in China to realize that with over a billion Chinese people on this planet, some of them were bound to have emigrated and lived outside the country?

'No, no, we're not Malay! As you may know, there's a substantial population of overseas Chinese in Malaysia!' Mother exclaimed, emphasizing the importance of using the term *Huaren* for Chinese rather than *Zhongguoren*, which meant citizen of China.

'Ah, well, you know, for us countryfolk in China, it's pretty hard to remember all that. To us, it's easier if all of you are Malays! Not Malaysian because of your new citizenship, but ethnically Malay!'

God. I wasn't sure if I really needed a smoke, or whether I just really wanted to punch this guy. Didn't he know that there were Chinese settlers throughout Southeast Asia, a greater part of which was the Han ethnic group that journeyed to the Nanyang over the last 300 years?

I thought I'd speak, but my mother wasn't done just yet.

'Yes, I see your point. But bear in mind, our ancestors from the southern provinces didn't sail across the South China Sea as mere Han Chinese people. When they left China, they began a historic journey as Hua migrants, as Huaqiao, who held their head high in the face of adversity for they were the dominant ethnicity amongst the great diversity of Chinese ethnicities. Our passports might not be the same maroon colour as yours, but who are you to say that we Malaysian Chinese are not part of the *Zhonghua minzu*?'

I was impressed that she said all of this calmly and so factually. I would've probably lost my rag.

'Oh no, auntie . . . I wasn't saying that, please don't misunderstand. It's just that I've had overseas Chinese passengers who've expressed the very opposite opinion! They only wanted to be identified as Huaren, as mere human beings who happened to be of Chinese ethnicity, and nothing more. They want nothing to do with China or any of our values, it seems,' Wang Shifu said, eyes unwavering from the road ahead throughout all of this.

'Where were they from, those passengers?' I asked.

'Singaporeans mostly!' said the shifu.

Now I needed a drink too.

Forty-five minutes of driving later, we found ourselves rolling down a winding slope into Betelnut Valley. It wasn't quite lunch time yet, but right after we parked, I felt massive hunger pangs,

and so I told Mother to go ahead with Wang Shifu to begin the
tour of the heritage park, while I made for the food court not far
past the ticketing booth. Inside, four kinds of food were offered
from all around the island, advertised as having gimmicky north,
south, east and west origins. I opted for the one noodle dish with
the 'time-honoured' signage; I don't remember in which part of
the island it was first concocted, only that it wasn't very good.

After eating my fill, I still thought about having that drink
but, as the waiters told me, it turned out the only alcohol served
at Betelnut Valley, one of the handful of AAAA (China rates its
tourist attractions with a number of A(s)) national tourist attractions
in China, was rice wine fermented by the indigenous Li and Miao
people of Hainan Island. So I exited the canteen and made for
the gift shop area, where tea-cup-sized servings of the sweet and
tangy alcoholic beverage were given out for the tourists to sample
by the promoters, who were dressed in black-and-red, woven, tribal
attire; and were made available to purchase by the bottle or dozen,
depending on how much you could drink, or in my mother's case—
how many bottles she could sneak through Malaysian customs
before having to slip a little something to the officer on duty.

I gulped down two cups and politely declined any more. If
I could be completely honest with the promoter, I would've told
her I was much more interested in the Li traditional dress she was
wearing, an intricately woven pattern of angular shapes embroidered
with multicoloured, yarn-dyed fabric. I found out later that those
traditional garments were up for sale too—albeit far inferior in its
design and detailing—as souvenirs at the gift shop, where one could
also bring home other pieces of commoditized Miao or Li culture.

Among the shimmering display were teapots and cups,
alongside bowls, decorative plates and carved chopsticks. As I
walked the floor, it became apparent that these were only a few
among what seemed like a complete catalogue of every kind of
silverware and jewellery imaginable, displayed in tiny stores and

booths of sandalwood furnishing which, coupled with the teak flooring, lent the entire floor the feeling as if you were in a giant treehouse. I picked out a silver bracelet from the jewellery box, and thought that of all the women I knew, Rei could probably make it work best. Except that, when I thought of her now, I couldn't put a face to her name, and all I remembered was that she liked to dress up and was fun to be around, her natural air of blossoming-from-girl-into-woman which she exuded being what drew me towards her most.

What was it that I actually knew about Rei, or any of the other women I met on dating apps for that matter? Knowing their name, what they did for work, and what they liked to wear was one thing; but as to understanding who they were as human beings, I fell hopelessly short. Being Chinese and able to speak Mandarin meant little when I was in essence a foreigner in this country—one who was able to penetrate the iridescent bubble of Chinese life, only to linger at the outermost surface of its societal subjectivity. Perhaps because they saw me as someone who resembled them only insofar as my ethnicity and spoken language were concerned, but not as an out-and-out Zhongguoren who bled red, even more so than I already did when wounded.

An ethnic Li sales assistant approached me with a smile. She had a fairer complexion than most of the tribespeople working at Betelnut Valley. With her neatly combed bangs she looked as Han as one could be, except for her pair of big, deep-set eyes and broad forehead. She got behind the counter and asked if I would like to try on the bracelet I had been holding unknowingly for some time now. I felt obliged and nodded.

'That one's too small for you,' she said, and from a wooden box she pulled out a cuff bracelet with a triangular engraving, a minimally designed piece which allowed the shape and beauty of the silver to stand out.

'I think this suits you very well,' she said as I clamped together the ends of the bracelet over my wrist, not breaking her smile the whole time.

'Do you think it would suit a foreigner too?'

'Umm . . . that depends. What gender and how tall? And where is your friend from?'

'It's for me. I'm from Malaysia.'

'I see. Oh, you're one of those overseas Chinese! Are you here on Aynam for travel?'

I just loved the way she pronounced Hainan in the local dialect.

'I'm here for a xungen trip actually . . . my ancestors were from here.'

'Oh! You're a fellow Hainanese clan member then, deserving of a warm, *Lizu* welcome now that you've come back to your *laojia!* Are you going to the bamboo-dance ceremony?'

'That depends. Will you be doing the dance?'

'No, not today, but some really hot aunties will be!'

'Guess it's my lucky day.'

'It may well be. Wearing that silver bracelet, you'll have all the good fortune of our people with you, at all times.'

'You promise?'

'Promise.'

Running my fingers over the greyish-white engravings gave me a strange sensation, something in between security, satisfaction and silliness. I was able to appreciate the fine craftsmanship of the indigenous Li people with every touch of the subtly engraved grooves on the bracelet, where reflected dull within its polished surface, was the silhouette of one of their most beautiful women gazing back at me.

Having it on sure felt good.

'Does this come with a free gift?' I asked, reaching for my wallet.

'Where have you been?' Mother asked, getting up from the log bench at the centre of the tribal courtyard where the crowd was dispersing, 'You just missed the erhu ensemble and the man playing the nose flute! They say his range is over three octaves!'

'I ate and did a little bit of shopping. Shouldn't chromatic range be predetermined by the range of the instrument itself?'

'I don't know, son, but it sure was impressive! Did you see the old ladies knitting those yarns, with their feet pressed firm against the wooden poles? I'm certain that's the same fabric they use for their traditional collarless dress. Absolutely lovely! What did you buy?'

I showed her the bracelet in the box. She looked unimpressed, which was oddly unusual of her.

'What's this supposed to be?'

'A silver bracelet, Ma. Don't you find these intricate carvings cool?' I asked, pointing them out to her lest she missed them.

'They're all right, I guess . . . but what is it?'

'What do you mean? It's a bracelet, you put it on your wrist and hope for the best.'

'I mean, what are the tribal beliefs associated with wearing it? Is it supposed to bring you luck or wealth? Maybe safeguard and watch over you on your travels?'

'I don't know, Ma. I just like the way it looks on me. It would be best if it exponentially reduced my repellence of women, or not add to it at the very least.'

'It's not a magic bracelet, son. Even the tribespeople know that much.'

'Never mind, dear Mother. We must remember that one has to deny knowledge in order to make room for faith.'

'What . . .? Are you quoting Mao or something?'

'It's Kant, Ma.'

'All right, all right. Believe what you want, you don't have to start swearing, okay? Let's go look for Wang Shifu. He left quite some time ago for *one* cigarette.'

'Maybe he meant one pack.'

The erhu and nose flute ensemble of the Li people gathered for another performance just as we were leaving the courtyard. No soundcheck or tune-up was necessary for the elderly flute quartet and erhu trio, only a few claps from the conductor and they were on their way, playing a predominantly pentatonic melody in shrill, nasally dissonance. The all-male line-up was fluid and played flawlessly for all I could fathom. I wondered if they were lauded as rockstars within the community of tribespeople, and whether or not they possessed tendencies to accidentally OD on betel nut or rice wine, possibly even have their own access to groupies?

The music gradually faded as we climbed the stone steps leading to a lookout point where we stopped, allowing ourselves a moment to take in the limitless, green cultivation of palm and coconut trees stretching across the vast acres below us. Into the horizon the verdant foliage melded into hues of crimson and aquamarine, approaching the great grey ocean set ablaze by a westward-moving sun that induced the mildest of melancholias, subtle and almost abstract, until one gave in to the sheer power of the sublime before them.

It was hard for me to imagine a life on Hainan Island. It was hard to imagine myself staying in China for much longer.

Mother and I stood watching the invisible wind rustle through the coconut estate, a scene reminiscent of our many drives through the palm-oil estates of Parit Yaani en route to Yong Peng during my childhood. I knew she wanted me to go back to Malaysia, even if it meant I wasn't home by her side; somewhere or anywhere in the same country would be good enough.

She didn't have to say a word. There was already too much expressed in the unsaid.

We found Wang Shifu catching forty winks in the reclined driver's seat, snoring with his feet lifted high on to the dashboard. After two light slaps of his face, he started the engine, and proceeded to drive us northeast for another two hours until we reached the city of Wenchang, blaring his horn every time he wanted to pass any vehicle blocking our path on the highway.

We got there a little past dinner time, tired, hungry and a tiny bit more deaf than when we had started out thanks to the incessant honking along the way. Wang Shifu suggested we get the duck dry pot, which didn't sound so bad until he explained that the dish consisted mostly of duck heads and duck feet topped with chilli and coriander.

'Doesn't sound all that appetizing,' I remarked.

'I know, right? I don't digest coriander particularly well,' Mother whispered, before arching her head forward, 'Shifu, how about some Wenchang chicken? Know any local haunts nearby?'

'Oh yes, of course . . . I forgot you might want to try that as tourists. Be warned though, the chicken here are tough, and they don't chew as easy as the Hainanese chicken you serve in Southeast Asia.'

'Can't be any chewier than duck head.'

'Or feet.'

And so, we sat down to eat at the farmhouse restaurant on the outskirts of Wenchang, a family establishment where service was conducted at its own leisurely pace. Wang Shifu was quick to inform us of the fact that this restaurant had once featured on national television in its heyday, as was apparent from the many banners which read 'hundred-year-old shop' and 'CCTV featured' emblazoned all over its façade, tokens from yesteryear flaunted with pride by the owners who, of course, happened to be buddies with our driver.

Wang Shifu did our ordering for us and after drinking a couple of rounds of beer with everyone, we were served an oily platter of poached chicken on a rustic plate, one that was only surpassed in grease by the establishment's grimy, tiled flooring. Tiny saucers with chilli and my mother's favourite coriander were given to us as a dipping sauce for our chicken, but what we really missed was the blended Hainanese chilli served in Malaysia. With my very first bite I almost broke a tooth chowing down on the island's signature chicken.

'The taste is in its toughness,' the master warned. 'On Hainan we only serve the most organic chicken from the mountain farms!'

We dug into our food and the table talk died down, and only Wang Shifu spoke to order more stir-fried vegetables or beer. We devoured the chopped-up bird before us voraciously, eventually leaving only the claws of the phoenix and its head in the middle of the plate.

'In China, people usually fight over the head. But with you Malaysians, you don't even touch it!'

'Please, Shifu, you go ahead. You've driven us the whole, long day,' Mother offered.

'I will leave it for the young man who works in the big city, he will need the chicken brain for the soundness of mind, for the peacefulness of his dreams!'

'It does all that?' I asked, tapping the tips of the chopsticks on the tabletop and reaching for the head.

'And more! It's good for your virility!'

Everything seemed to be good for one's virility in China.

Mother gave me a look. *You wouldn't dare.*

With the gnarled wooden chopsticks, I clasped the slimy head of the chicken and lifted it into my mouth. Feeling its cold skin and every orifice against my tongue, I manoeuvred its tender little skull between my teeth and bit down with a loud crack.

I didn't taste anything special, but it was too late for any dipping sauce.

After dinner, Wang Shifu dropped us off at a hotel in Wenchang before going to stay at the drivers' hostel by himself. Utterly fatigued from the day's travel, Mother and I turned in for an early night immediately after checking in, although before we knew it, morning had come for us once more and after breakfast, we again found ourselves waiting in a hotel lobby for Wang Shifu and his van.

Mother told shifu the address of our ancestral shrine and after he plugged it into the GPS, we were soon on our way towards Pokou Village on the western outskirts of Wenchang. As opposed to the day before, hardly anyone talked as we drove there, which I thought made this pilgrimage back to the ancestral home appropriately solemn.

I found myself watching the endless stretch of palm-oil trees, wondering what life on Hainan Island would've been like a hundred years ago, even though in my mind I couldn't imagine anything other than an opaque darkness brought on by poverty and civil war. During that period in time, people would have left Hainan Island to work as chefs or kitchen hands in colonial Malaya, unable to ever return to their homeland under the communist rule. I felt something move within me when I realized that, although the rich history of diaspora was plain for me to comprehend, the circumstances of its particular reality remained completely obscure and inconceivable to me.

After about an hour's driving, we left the freeway and turned into an unpaved gravel road leading to the village, which I soon realized, as Wang Shifu stopped to interrupt some uncles' late morning chitchat on their motorcycles in front of their clay houses for directions, was in fact already the village itself. I sat up from my slouched position and looked around across the muddy, red road. There were two buildings built about ten metres apart, one being the Pokou Village Committee Building and the other being the Pokou Village Public Toilet.

'I'm looking for the Zhou ancestral shrine,' Wang Shifu said, after winding down his window.

'Ah yes, yes. You've come to the right place. Welcome to Pokou! Are you a Zhou descendent?' asked the half-naked man on a motorcycle.

'No, my surname is Wang, but, these two good folk are. They're Hainanese from Malaysia.'

'From Malaysia! Just two? The last time we had a bus full of visitors from a Hainanese Association in Malaysia.'

'Well, the ones I bring you today are mother and son. Could you show us the way?'

The shirtless man gestured for us to wait, before calling somebody on his phone.

Within five minutes, a man considerably more dressed than the others showed up riding a motorcycle. He had greying hair and the same teak-tanned Hainanese complexion as all the men there. We got down to shake his hand.

'My name is Zhou Chang Ren, the Chang being *flourishing*, and the Ren being *benevolence*,' said the man wearing a white, nylon shirt with its sleeves rolled to the elbows.

'Our surname is Zhou too, or Chew in Hainanese,' said Mother, telling him our names.

'That's wonderful. We're all of the same clan then! My surname is Zhou, your surname is Zhou, and the same goes for this guy, this guy and this guy. All Zhou,' said Mr Zhou, pointing to the shirtless men on their bikes.

The weather was sultry and perfect for shirtlessness.

We followed Mr Zhou's motorcycle through a narrow, twisty road lined with coconut trees and into a clearing where a vast cultivation of paddy fields stretched out from either side of the van, and in the soggy troughs of ploughed earth one could see the reflection of the clouds looming in the distance.

We drove up a small hill and came to a halt in front of a shrine built on top of a red mound of earth, the old stone steps leading up to it covered with the weeds which grew out through the cracks. Up there on its landing was a towering swallowtail roof gate, with the words *Zhou's Ancestral Hall* written in faded ink calligraphy from right to left across its arch.

We climbed the steps and passed through the gates into the ascetic courtyard, where a sense of dignity permeated the air even in its current dilapidated and decrepit state. The concrete pavement had turned black from years of being saturated with water and dirt, and the grass was sparse with weeds having taken over the garden. In the corner, was an austere and weather-beaten outhouse for the groundskeeper's use.

Mother turned to me. *We're here*, she said.

I felt the hot wind blow right through me, across the red earth and to the blue sea.

'Yes, we're here,' I said.

Mr Zhou unlocked the door to the main hall, and showed us in.

On our left, was an altar covered with ancestral plaques, detailing the names of the first Han settlers in Hainan Island some 800 years ago at the turn of the 13th century. To our right, was a red plaque of modern times, containing the names of current Zhou clan members who had made a donation towards the upkeep of the ancestral shrine. On the walls were various murals of cranes taking flight during spring, alongside poets gazing wistfully across the West Lake and gods crossing the rivers in a lotus.

At the centre, was a large painting of a man named Zhou Xiu Mei, who was born as Song Jin Shi in Quanzhou, Fujian province. The artwork depicted him fleeing south in the aftermath of the Jingkang incident, which saw Emperor Gaozong of Song move the capital south from Bianjiang to Lin'an—present day Hangzhou. Eventually, Song Jin Shi came to Qiongshan on Hainan Island, where he then changed his name to Zhou Xiu Mei. Nothing is known about his original familial ancestry in Fujian and he is remembered through this shrine that is his namesake and legacy.

Mr Zhou tapped me on the shoulder to pass me a burning incense, which I knelt down to insert into the incense pot very awkwardly.

'Would you like to have a look at the family name tree?'

I stood up and nodded. Mr Zhou pointed to the far side of the wall, where a tattered scroll of calligraphy bore the names from the 11th to the 64th generation. My eyes traced and settled on mine. I was of the 29th generation—the middle name was Jia, which meant *home*.

We thanked Mr Zhou and said goodbye. Mother passed him a small envelope to show our gratitude.

'To be able to come to China to discover your roots like this . . . Xungen—it's a kind of happiness, isn't it?' asked Wang Shifu, as we were leaving the hall.

I didn't reply. He couldn't see it, but I was nodding in agreement. My mind was elsewhere, thinking about the steel door handle I saw at the entrance to the shrine, with the words *chu ru ping an* engraved on the face of the lotus.

Peace when you come and go.

Peace wherever you may go.

Chapter 12

WHYAMI: There's still so much I don't understand.

sappho31: What about?

WHYAMI: China. Then there's the world outside China, and you.

sappho31: What brings this sudden insight?

WHYAMI: Nothing in particular. But I've decided to stop using dating apps for a while.

sappho31: So you've finally decided to live like a poet.

WHYAMI: Like Rimbaud?

sappho31: More or less, one who is not afraid of loneliness.

WHYAMI: I don't know about that, but I've deactivated my accounts.

sappho31: Ah, okay. I read your article on ShanghaiPRIDE though. I thought it was . . . an interesting perspective from a man.

WHYAMI: . . . how did you know that was me? I never told you about the article.

sappho31: You mentioned it before. You tell everyone everything. You were working for an SNS company as an English content writer, remember? There aren't that many in Shanghai. All I had to do was ask my foreigner friends what they were reading, et voila!

WHYAMI: Still though, how did you know which article was written by me?

sappho31: Who else would consider *whyamiWaimai* a good pseudonym?

WHYAMI: Ha! Ha! I was hoping you had recognized my distinct writing style, the existential yet humorous.

sappho31: You make me feel existential. What I'd give to know what's going on in that head of yours.

WHYAMI: I could say the same about you. Me? I'm not that complicated. I'm usually busy separating absurd from real but, more and more I realize there's no point.

sappho31: The real is the absurd, Camus had already proven that.

WHYAMI: Camus was a nihilist at heart.

sappho31: Even though he wrote against nihilism precisely?

WHYAMI: He may have, but . . . as a response, absurdism and its morals bring no more joy to one's life than nihilism would.

sappho31: Even if that were the case, what do you gain from picking apart the absurd from the real? It would still be a deeply nihilistic act at the end of the day.

WHYAMI: By separating absurd from real, I gain an uninhibited access to pure thoughts. Thoughts that drive a subject to commit specific acts, in other words . . . I would be able to see clearly that, without the real, life is just kind of stupid.

sappho31: Really? Is that your conclusion?

WHYAMI: Yes, it is.

sappho31: You should write and get published.

WHYAMI: I would. But you wouldn't want to read it anyway.

sappho31: You never know, you don't know me. I guess I can't say I really know you either.

WHYAMI: No, I don't think you ever wanted to know me.

Chapter 13

I sank into deep depression after getting back to Shanghai.

I thought it might be the return to the intermittent spells of rain and the biting cold, or the abrupt disappearance of the scorching sun from my life once more. I wasn't sure. Being back in the hustle and bustle of Shanghai was unsettling, but only for about five minutes. I found even the gloom of winter, which had settled in by the time I got back, to be quite acceptable once I got a scarf and a few more layers on.

Somehow, for reasons lost beyond the realm of better words, I could feel a sheer bitterness beginning to take over my life, and there was little I could do to resist it.

Mother had bid goodbye to me and to China, before boarding the plane for Kuala Lumpur from Haikou Airport. She called me as soon as she reached home, already into the wee hours of the next day. By then, I too had gotten off my plane and had travelled back to my apartment in Shanghai, where I whiled away the time without unpacking but sipping on a beer with my feet on top of the cast-iron heater against the wall.

Just as she had done during my time away from home at university, Mother asked if I was back in my room, as if I had anywhere better to be other than editing articles in front of my computer, tap-tapping away the hours until dawn. She asked if I'd had fun on our trip. I nodded as I said yes, like she could see me. Mother thanked me for accompanying her on the xungen trip.

I thought of thanking her back for footing the bill for the bulk of our expenses on Hainan Island. I felt I ought to have been the one who had paid for the trip, like any self-respecting adult would do for their mother. But the reality was, I couldn't, having to return to Shanghai and the weight of its living costs.

As a sort of return favour, I promised to meet a son of her friend, who had recently moved to Shanghai from Johor. She said that he might need help settling in, maybe even some assistance in finding a job or somewhere to stay. This wasn't something I was all that keen on doing, but I acquiesced. I told her I would see what I could do, all the while hoping that I wouldn't have to do anything more than meet up with this guy for a cup of coffee.

Being the good son that I was, I let a couple of weeks go by before completely forgetting about the whole thing, until I got a WeChat friend request from a guy named KenSon late one evening with a message saying that his parents wouldn't let him exist in peace until he made contact with me.

'So how about we meet for dinner tonight?' I asked over text.

'Dinner, huh? Didn't know my parents were setting me up. How does drinks later tonight on Nanjing Lu sound? If you're hungry there's always *yakitori*.'

I said okay, and went to take a shower before leaving my apartment for the day. I hoped he was paying for the yakitori.

Having submitted in my latest assignments early, I had a rare free day all to myself. I had been operating at an unprecedented level of efficiency of late, going from research to first draft in no more than a few hours regardless of the topic I worked on: a list detailing the many marathons being held from autumn through to winter; off-grid living in western China; and the newest independent breweries in the Shanghai craft-beer scene— all topics I could finish in a day if not late into the wee hours of the following morning. Most of the articles were minimally edited by the subeditors when published and if any changes were made to them at all, I barely noticed. A comma here and there, long sentences split in half and moved around for quicker reading, maybe an addition of double-angle brackets for book or film titles—a Chinese practice I could never quite wrap my head around.

I was at a loss about what to do. After running on cups of magic and americano for two weeks straight, the last thing I wanted was to spend the morning unwinding with caffeine and pouring over a novel I would forget in a fraction of the time it would take to read it. So I walked past the row of cafés down Ferguson Lane, past the Instagrammers and WeChat bloggers standing over their tables with their cameras mounted on gimbals which they held so deftly, assisting the balancing and shooting of would-be content that would hopefully propel one in the direction of Internet fame, or at the very least, towards some kind of relevance floating at the very surface of the sea of mediocrity across the World Wide Web. I walked past the hipster bookstore that refused to sell any of their used books, that glorified, second-hand, hangout spot where you sipped on over-frothed lattes while having one too many smokes in the garden. But such was the way of the Bohemian who collected plethoras of books and periodicals in languages they could barely fathom as dilettantes, who knew the history of the writers better than the historic gestures their works represented and who, through their lifestyles, upheld the significance of being authentic over the authenticity of significant being.

Over two months had passed since my chance encounter with Sofia, the girl who had unwittingly caused me to stop smoking cigarettes after our first and only night out together. Our exchanges that followed were brief and perfunctory to say the least, having both agreed that we should meet again although we never did. There were times I wanted to share the news of my newfound abstinence from cigarettes with her but felt that there was no real point in texting her out of the blue like that.

On a certain day of a certain month, I wondered how she was doing. I wondered whether or not she had finished her advanced Mandarin course—which I had been surprised she had enrolled into when she moved back to Shanghai in the first place, because it just seemed so redundant for someone so much like a local already—and whether or not she had accepted that position of draughtswoman as a last resort for work, or whether she had chosen to pursue postgraduate studies in architecture that she said was what she felt she really wanted.

Whether or not she was even in the country still.

Today was such a day where I found myself thinking about her, but that was always as far as it went.

I continued my march against the cold of winter and the faint, mocking glow of sunlight; trotting past the grand Wukang mansions seized from the bourgeois during the cultural revolution, scornfully repartitioned and repurposed for a cramped and communal living, only to be re-gentrified by the new, socialistic-capitalistic bourgeois of today.

On my walk, I saw throngs of people queuing outside in the freezing cold for ice cream, amongst them Lemtosh-wearing foreigners with their Chinese girlfriends in UGG boots and pantyhose, university girls in Supreme sweaters not lifting their gaze from their cell phones. There was a young father standing on a two-wheeled electric scooter smoking a cigarette, his toddler in baby Yeezies right beside him. In winter, the streets of Xuhui were lent an extra dimension of the poetic, with tall, leafless sycamore casting shadows on to stores that could not contain their own individualism. The French Concession was the perfect place for travellers to congregate, be it the foreigners or the drifters visiting from outside Shanghai, who would mingle with the octogenarian uncles engrossed in epic battles of Chinese chess by the roadside, and the surly aunties who only left their houses for the market or the Mahjong parlour.

I ended up getting a coffee after all, and went on to spend the afternoon sitting on a bench, watching the lives of others coming and going in a steady flux on Wukang Lu, feeling that soon I too would be part of this ebb and flow of people, but would anyone watch me go then? Flux was change, and change was good.

If life was supposed to be like clockwork, then I might as well be the dirt between cogs in need of oiling. I needed to move on with my life. I was desperate to be away from the cold, and the rapid iciness enfolding me.

Even on the dark, misty street the son of my mother's friend looked awfully familiar.

KenSon stood at about 168 cm, was clothed in denim overalls, washed almost entirely of its indigo, and a chambray western shirt in black, complete with a ferocious tiger embroidered across its back panel, which I would later deem to be almost as ugly as he was. His midwestern-farm outfit was further accentuated by feather pendants and a pair of commando-soled brogue boots, which only enhanced his stockiness and the overall effect of making him appear simultaneously tall and short.

As I approached, he tossed the cigarette he had been smoking to the ground to shake my hand, and from a red pack of Zhonghwa he extracted another to proffer to me.

I refused; he lit up.

'My mother warned that you might be a bit of a killjoy,' he smirked.

We spent the night drinking beer and chewing on skewers at an *izakaya*, but the flow of our conversation was stagnant at best. KenSon didn't remember me at all, but I figured it would be easier to not bring that to light. After all, I didn't remember his real name either.

'Is KenSon your real name?'

'Of course not. It's Tony, Tony Leong,' he said, exhaling smoke and reaching for the chicken liver.

'Tony Leung . . . the actor Waizai himself? Is that why you smoke?'

'Maybe just call me KenSon, now eat your chicken.'

I picked up the skewer of lightly charred liver chunks, lifted it up under the light of the counter to admire its transparent glaze and caramelized edges, before sliding it into my mouth.

'Good, isn't it?'

'It's like chewing on chicken butter.'

'Here, have another beer.'

This guy managed to pop open a bottle of Qingdao with his chopsticks and handed it to me. *GANBEI!* we shouted, and in a few hurried gulps we each finished a whole bottle. We ordered more beer, and yet more beer.

KenSon lit up and started puffing on another cigarette. From certain angles behind the shroud of smoke, I guess he did look a little like Tony Leung, with his slicked-back hair.

I reached for the pack, tapped its bottom a few times and pulled one out. The white-and-brown-tipped Zhonghwas reminded me very much of the Marlboros that Luna used to pose with in her pictures. I put one between my lips, flicked the lighter and inhaled.

At times, when the pauses found me in my life, I would often meditate and ruminate on this grotesque thing called desire, to the point that I pulverized the very idea of it to a pulp.

Slow and fickle flame, oughtn't it to burn mindlessly, like fire licking through a dry wilderness? The evening breeze could only entreat it so much, before sending any inkling of desire rippling through the lalang and fading away, leaving me in the wake of its arid wind. Faceless, invisible, intangible. A thief in the night, abandoning me as soon as it knew there was nothing it could take.

But then there was also a desire like KenSon's at variance with mine, a difference as clear and as blindingly brilliant as day; and if anyone were there to glimpse it, it would surely leave them reeling in a daze.

Our conversation died down, we had both allowed it to run its course. At nobody's suggestion, we left the yakitori establishment, and the moment we stepped outside I began to feel a good buzz from the alcohol and cigarettes. Every step we took down Nanjing Road felt directionless, if only serving to take us farther and farther away from the cold. I felt like a being completely present in the moment, one newly found in his rapturous haze, taking in the neon lights that cascaded in from the red-light district, the forceful grabbing of passers-by and the spittle-in-your-face hard-selling done by the pimps.

Yes, I'm familiar with the concept. *No*, I don't want to try one of your girls down in the water.

'What's the harm? A man who has never been down in the water knows not where the mermaids swim!' KenSon smirked.

'Now this is a man who knows what he wants! A real cowboy taking life by the reins!' one of the pimps yelled.

'If you feel the pressing need to call me something, I'd much prefer "farm boy" over "cowboy",' he says and flashes me a wide grin, before vanishing into the hotel with the sweet-talking pimp.

I followed suit. Not so much overcome with desperation to 'get down in the water', but because I was subdued by the urge to pass some water of my own.

In through a set of opaque glass doors I scrambled, and with every passing second, I neared bursting point in my lower abdomen. Never in my life had I wanted to take a leak so bad, apparently having pictures of call girls shoved in my face did that to me, which I thought was really funny, and started giggling like an idiot as I stumbled past the empty lobby and down a flight of stairs. When I regained my balance, KenSon was already out of sight. How far ahead could the amphibious farm boy have gone?

I pushed on down the musty hallway, that was so filled with dusty crates and boxes that it didn't appear as vacant as it was deserted. I had been resisting the urge to just unzip my pants and relieve myself right then and there on the cardboard boxes, but I wasn't strong enough to do it any longer. Moments later, I was smoking a cigarette with one hand and holding my penis with the other. In the narrow, underground passageway, I stood alone, trickling urine on to the flat cardboard boxes that darkened as soon they were drenched in yellow piss.

For the first time in a long time, I felt at peace.

But there was no escaping the all-seeing eye and when I finished, I looked up to see a spherical CCTV with its pinhole camera obscured behind dark plastic.

'What the hell are you looking at?'

'Just in case it wasn't clear, I'd spit at you if I could.'

'D'you know where my . . . friend went?'

'He's my only . . . he's the only one who knows I'm here.'

'I need to know the way out.'

'Is there any way out from all of this?'

Did you take it? a loud voice crackled from above just as the doors of the lift slid open.

Startled, I lost my footing and stumbled out of the cauldron of eau de second-hand smoke, right into what appeared to be a traditional Chinese foyer of sorts. The lighting was warm although a little dim, the few pieces of furniture teak but tacky.

I looked around for the source of the voice but found no one. Had the voice come from the lift's speakers?

Then the voice came on again, this time more commanding and less muffled than before.

Come forward. Through the circular entrance to your left, all the way down to the pixiu statue.

I swayed down the hallway. Was it real marble that my sneakers were squeaking on?

Stop, stop, stop!

I came to a halt. Sure enough on each side of the altar were two pixiu statues in faux-gold, both with their mouths agape and gaze angled towards the heavens or, in this case, the Jiangshan fresco painting on the other side of the wall.

Hey, over here.

The pixiu was talking to me.

I couldn't possibly be that drunk?

Crouching down, I caressed the head of the dragon-lion on the left.

'You want to swallow all my money and keep it there forever in your anus, don't you? Well . . . the joke's on you cause I'm just another poor ass motherfucker! Hardly have enough to cover rent . . . in fact, the only way I'm getting back home tonight is to leg it. What do you say to that?' I yelled.

The beast didn't respond. Was I really expecting it to talk?

I waited a little longer. As I examined the statue, I discovered the hidden intercom wedged in the pixiu's mouth, behind its protruding fangs.

Then came a loud clank from behind me, like the sound of a lever detaching.

When I turned around, he was already standing there, in a white bathrobe and rubber slippers—Farm boy Tony Leung, puffing on his damn cigarette as usual, except this time with wet, let down hair.

'News flash: my piss smells like cigarette ash. Did you know that was possible?' asked the dickhead formerly known as KenSon.

I didn't reply. Who intentionally sniffs their urine?

'That was fun to watch,' he continued, 'Did you really think a statue could talk?'

'Nice robe, *shabi*.'

'I didn't scare you, did I? Come on in, I've been waiting long enough.'

He stepped in front of the fresco painting of the Jiangshan, and with the press of a button concealed within its mossy greenery, brought half the mountain and waterfall swinging inward.

At this point there was only one way forward, and so into the brilliant, white light we stepped.

When Raymond Carver penned his second book of poetry, *When Water Comes Together with Other Water*, I was certain he would not have conceived of the element in the way that KenSon did.

Our journey through the veil of the waterfall and into KenSon's oasis began with a rather subdued greeting from the wistful-eyed pimp behind the counter who, in his black coveralls and white, jersey tee, jolted up shaking his head so violently, it put his canvas skullcap in a precarious position.

Had he been wearing this outfit all along? Was this even the same guy who had harried us in at the entrance?

'Evidently not all people are capable of following instructions. How hard is it to just follow behind us and not piss up our walls?' sighed the pimp.

'Relax, Big Panda, he's new here, a little piece of fresh meat for the girls.'

'Relax? Fuck me, I'm perfectly relaxed! You know, you're not the one who has to go back and forth through that musty hallway to bring in customers every hour of the day. You boys ready or what?'

'Just hold on to your overalls,' said the farm boy to the disgruntled railroad worker, before turning towards me. Without warning, he fished out a sealed pack of pills and thrust them towards me.

I looked at the pills and back at him again in confusion.

'What is this? Viagra?'

He smirked condescendingly. 'It's better than Viagra, it makes you more alert and spunky, if you will. Hey, if you don't like pills, I can get it in soluble powder form too—it tastes great. Just don't snort it, okay? One time a friend of mine did that and he got a hard-on, right in the nose!'

I didn't know if he was being serious but, as with many things he would say to me, I just took his word for it. I extracted a pill and swallowed it.

'Wow, you didn't even need water. That's hard-core, man! Trust me, your little brother will stand straighter than a flagpole in military camp.'

Come on. Why did he have to say military camp?

'I've only just met you, but you're dodgy as hell, you know that?'

'Relax, killjoy! It's not like we're doing anything wrong.'

'We aren't? This sure doesn't feel legal.'

'It's medicine! Don't get all authoritarian on me. People in Yunnan are doing hallucinatory mushrooms, putting them in soups and everything and nobody bats an eye! It's not as if we're doing ice or crystal meth, or anything like that.'

'Crystal meth is ice.'

'Aren't you a smartass? You-have-got-to-chill.'

'Sorry. I wouldn't mind some hallucinatory soup now, though.'

'No, you don't. You've taken the best kind of happy pill. It's perfectly legal too,' he winked.

'All right, boss . . .'

'Lighten up. Into reality we must project the fire we carry in our hearts, you get me?'

'Are you rainbow boys done?' the pimp chimed in. 'Listen, my dears, if it's ducks you want to see . . . well, of course, there's someone else I can call. Or, if you want a room, I could arrange that as well . . .'

'*Cao ni ma*. Bring out the mirror, then!'

'A mirror?'

'Yes, a figurative mirror. Imagine a piece of reality that mirrors the deepest desires within our hearts.'

'Wait. Isn't this from Harry Potter?'

'Don't interrupt me. Even primary school kids know how to raise their hands before asking questions. Listen, the mirror exists not merely to tantalize because whatever you see in the mirror will be offered to you; and if you can afford it, you may gaze into it anytime you want.'

I didn't quite follow but nodded anyway. Unlike KenSon, I wasn't born with an instruction manual for this thing called desire.

Nevertheless.

Big Panda feigned a smile, but the disdain in his eyes was beyond dissimulation. He mumbled into his smartphone, sending for the girls.

There I stood, on the cusp of reality, longing to project the fire within my heart into something.

I came around in a drunken haze with the weight of the world on top of me. I tried twisting and turning my body to find a more comfortable position, but it was a futile effort. Was this it for me? Would I be tied down by the weight of being forever?

'WHYAMIWaimai? Xiaogege, is that you?'

My eyes widened hearing the voice of a woman, who appeared to be straddling the lower half of my body, which was wrapped only with a towel. She on the other hand, was wearing nothing but a Doraemon helicopter hat.

'What are you wearing . . .?'

'Bamboo-copter! Don't you think it's cute?' teased the woman on top of me.

'No, I mean . . . why are you wearing that?'

'What do you mean. . . you don't like it? That's not what you said when you picked me out from the mirror, *gege.*'

What was all this about a mirror again?

I felt queasy and couldn't suppress a belch, it reeked of alcohol and smoky yakitori.

She got up, shaking her head, and went to grab a pack of red Marlboros from inside her sky-blue Doraemon suit hanging on the wall, which looked to be made of spandex. How could anyone fit into something so tight?

'Fuck this shit,' she said in one giant smoky exhalation. 'How many times have I told Big Panda that I don't ever want to take care of any blacked-out, drunk clients ever again? Yeah, I know I know, what choice do I have, right? Do you know how difficult it is to wash a barely conscious man, a drunk who stinks of alcohol and vomit at that?'

'We bathed . . .? You and me?'

She nodded and feigned a coquettish grin, her eyes open wide in disbelief.

'Yes. DingDang bathed you. You've got a very nicely shaped cock.'

Had she made me hard earlier? I wondered, looking down at my towel-covered crotch. Of course, it was now limp and flaccid.

DingDang edged closer towards me with every crossed step, her breasts modest and shapely with perky teats. They were so firm to the touch, and I was reminded of the sculpted breasts of the Goddess Aphrodite as a statue.

She was luscious with her thick, northern accent, fast with lots of erhua overtones, which many men wouldn't be bothered to fathom. I thought she sounded sexy and sophisticated, but even then I couldn't do it.

I watched her continue to stroke me, going down so hard and fast, but I just couldn't get it up.

This was pitiful.

'I think I should go. Don't worry, I'll still pay you, all right?'

She got up, looking almost insulted. But like a true professional, she quickly resumed her position of dominance before I could move even an inch. DingDang then began to rub her wetness against me with a virtuosity I had never experienced before.

'Big brother, by the time I'm done with you, no whore will ever have to hear your ugly words again,' she whispered.

It only occurred to me much later, when I was sober, that the prostitute named DingDang had called me WHYAMIWaimai, the pseudonym I used for all my articles written for *TRIESTE*.

How peculiar.

Even if she were the most avid follower of our page, how the woman had come to make the association as to who I was, or what I looked like, was beyond me.

Could she have been a stalker? Maybe an overly keen reader of my work, perhaps?

'Don't flatter yourself,' said KenSon before wolfing down the piping hot xiaolongbao filled with crab in one mouthful. 'D'you honestly think she knows you just from your writing? What probably happened was . . .' he paused to ingest another bun, 'she went through your phone when you weren't looking. Never take your eyes off a whore, comrade! Unlike this baozi, you can't just chew on a lady while scrolling through your phone . . .'

If only the baozi were made bigger, so he'd keep quiet for longer.

But I guess he did have a point.

I did pass out, after all.

Did I really do it with a prostitute? If so, how?

'How was DingDang? She seemed all over you after you picked her out of the mirror.'

'She was all right. You know how it is.'

'Hmm sure . . . why did you pick her, though, out of all the girls? She didn't really have that great a rack, despite her push-up bra, you could tell . . . I guess you must be an ass guy?'

'I don't know. She was the one who picked me and voluntarily jumped on me.'

'Voluntarily? Jesus, you sure as hell don't know how this is supposed to work.'

'Well, we talked a lot, before and after we did it. That felt nice.'

'Oh nice, huh? Perhaps I'll give her a try next time, that is, if you don't mind.'

Why the hell would I mind?

'Go ahead if you want to. Whatever.'

KenSon looked at me, cigarette dangling from his chapped lips, like a zombie-cowboy hybrid.

'You didn't fuck her, did you?'

'What do you mean?' I hesitated. 'I was just thinking you might want to try a different girl, maybe one that wasn't so . . . straight out of a manga.'

'You little virgin, wasting the courtesy of my money, the hospitality of my pills.'

'Don't be like this. Perhaps we could visit a different house next time.'

'Like hell would I waste another night of my life with you?'

'Come on, we'll find a cowboy-themed whorehouse.'

'Yeah, right! I'd love to, but I can't really do that.'

'Why not?'

'Most places have me . . . sort of . . . blacklisted.'

'All throughout Shanghai? Didn't you just arrive here?'

He nodded as he exhaled, putting yet another one out in the ashtray, a genocide of brown cigarette buds.

'There was a time in the past when I went too far with a few girls, but I don't regret what I did. I've actually been in Shanghai for a long time, your mother just didn't know about it.'

'Kinky. What could you have done to outrage the modesty of a whore?'

'You know how busy one can get in this city. You work overtime, barely have time to order Waimai, let alone eat it, then there's appearances to keep up, acquaintances and contacts with whom you have to socialize and work up a rapport, events you have to attend just so your boss knows that you went, even though they can't be bothered about it themselves.'

'I didn't know you were that busy. What do you do again?'

'Why do you always ask what's not important. Always pay attention to the crux of the matter! It's no wonder you have trouble with women.'

'Come on, serious question.'

'I've dabbled in the performing arts, if you must know. On and off. It's a kind of love-hate relationship. Happy now? No more questions on this matter.'

'My apologies, teacher. Go on, then, before the sun comes up and sobers you.'

'It's not like it's that big a deal anyway. I used to call in some girls regularly, you know, over to my apartment to take care of me on a weekly basis. And after a while, it got a little too customary . . . well, no, that would be a euphemism; in truth, it was mind-numbingly boring. I couldn't even get hard any more; so I did what any man would do, I asked the captain if any of his girls would like to fly double.'

'And they blacklisted you for that?'

'Don't be silly. It was because, out of curiosity one day, I decided to see how far I could push them to meet my necessities. So . . . I made them clean my apartment before we had sex.'

'You hired call girls to serve as your pay-by-the-hour maids?'

'Exactly. Before the sex.'

'You're kidding. Wouldn't they just refuse and leave?'

'Technically they can't. Say if I told them that the act of cleaning certain objects was the only real fetish that gets me going . . . a minimal level of service is required on their part,' he laughed. A joke, obviously this guy was.

'A scumbag's road to the call-girl blacklist—I could do an entire article for *TRIESTE* on that.'

'Ha! sure, like you would know anything about that. You didn't even do anything!'

Did I? Didn't I?

I forced a smile. The events of the last few hours remained submerged in a drunken muddle, and I was not too keen to revisit them. I wouldn't see KenSon for quite some time after our first night out.

Chapter 14

I know you didn't do it: so, won't you think about what I'm saying here? Without a doubt, you would have something to say if you had been inside DingDang.

I know you didn't think that I would know. Did you? You didn't do it.

The pills. How about the pills? You took them, right? Listen. Listen to me while you still can hear my voice. I'm telling you right here, right now, you've got a problem.

They don't want you! They don't want somebody so nice. Don't you think you're treating these girls with too much respect? That's why you can't get it up! That's right, I know. How do I know, you ask? Does it even matter? We're in China now. Who you are or what problems you have don't really matter. If you're not going to take the special pills of spring, you might as well give 'em back to me.

So, you did take them. Wow, and still you failed? Listen, at this point, I probably can't help, but just think about what I'm saying for a moment.

Who are you? Why the fuck are you even here? With so many people living in Shanghai, in China and in the world, it's hard for one to be completely by himself, isn't it? Moments and opportunities like these are scarce, so there's no excuse not to be yourself. The city always sees you, remember that—even with your melancholia in one step and weariness in the other.

Along with all of your loneliness, and the weight of living on your shoulders.

That has never made anyone special. Everyone knows this. You know this.

So why should you feel so special about your predicament?

Chapter 15

There were times in the past when I only wished for her to know what she meant to me. Now I just wished to forget; to achieve a complete erasure of the image and idea of her from my memory.

There was no cleaner way of wiping the slate than to write, as with every sentence I was able to obliterate, wash and move forward. At first, the writing would only trickle in, one word after the other. In these beginnings, I paid no heed to the reflective moment, unless there was absolutely no way of carrying on, which there always was. Soon, the words turned to lines and the lines turned to pages, and like the flow of river water gushing raw and free, the act of writing exonerated me.

The editor griped at my uninhibited prose, at once prone to sounding directionless as it was too free, to a point where it turned to becoming abstruse like an amateur version of the *Phenomenology of Spirit*, save being the good part.

But time has a way of clouding one's judgement, if only serving to blind that person momentarily so that they overlook flaws in something for no other reason than its having developed a familiarity in their eyes that it becomes misconstrued as something favourable. With every published article, the editor warmed up to my vehement style of delivery, and I grew more and more preoccupied with various styles of writing, especially intrigued by the new journalistic style of Gay Talese.

Or could I be a Joan Didion? No. Didion had a magical way of dealing with self-pity. I on the other hand, kind of needed it, almost relied on it as a kind of sustenance.

It occurred to me I had all but forgotten about Luna. Who was she but a distant memory now? Perhaps that was all she had ever been for me—an idea and a concept I could never wrap my head around.

That I should never try to wrap my head around.

I deleted all the dating apps that had littered my phone, removing one garish icon after another that only accentuated my loneliness whenever I opened them.

Decluttering. I liked it.

I had first heard of the word from Sofia, the first girl I had met on Tinder here in Shanghai. But perhaps 'heard' is a strong word, for all I had done was read an article she had shared on her WeChat moments, and from then onwards, I was inspired to implement some of the said mantras in my daily life.

Apart from the dating apps, I started getting rid of the garbage and clutter in my own apartment, which mainly constituted of the old newspapers and free magazines I had picked up around the city. I pulled out several black trash bags from the drawer and started to stuff some old pieces of clothing in them—mostly items I had brought over from Malaysia but had never worn because of the difference in weather and more importantly, the much more stylish demands of Shanghai vogue. I removed the plastic containers and cardboard packaging that had piled up around the kitchen, mostly as makeshift ashtrays or receipt depositories, and put them all into a clear, recycling bag. Then I added the books and CDs lying around my apartment to another bag, before I lost discipline and began to reach for everything I no longer wanted and threw them into the biggest bag I could find—one trash bag to rule them all, I figured.

At the end of the session, my room didn't so look so much decluttered as it looked empty. A mild feeling of satisfaction and accomplishment washed over me. However, this feeling of triumph lasted only as long as it took me to walk to the refuse room to dispose of my four plastic bags, for I realized that if it took me less than a half hour to declutter my room, I was only properly suited to be a minimalist insofar as I was poor.

Unconsciously too, I began to cut people from my life. The colleagues I didn't want to see after and outside of work, I ignored. The few acquaintances I had made from socializing around Shanghai, I avoided. With KenSon, though, it was more peculiar, for without any intention or effort on my part, the farm boy, Tony Leung, disappeared from my life. Just like that, he stopped replying on his WeChat account, and eventually deleted it.

Even though I had only met KenSon that one time, it appeared he wasn't one to vanish without a parting gift. Just as the dawn was about to bring our first meeting to an end and I was about to be finally free of the man, KenSon started going on about a package. *A package. I've sent you a package, so take care of it*, were his smoky parting words.

At the time, I had been completely drunk and wrung out from being out the whole night, and completely forgot about this thing about a package. A week or two went by, and just as I was about to assume I had dreamt the whole thing, I stumbled upon a parcel at my doorstep after returning from work one evening.

A box. Just a little bigger than a shoebox. Could KenSon have blessed me with one of those nice canvas shoes he was wearing with the Paradise Rubber Athletic Shoes logo at the back? Maybe a nice pair of denim overalls like the one he had been wearing?

Didn't think so. This was a little heavier than your typical shoebox, and a dull rattling sound could be heard when I shook it from side to side.

I slid my pocketknife into the lines of duct tape, sealed so clean and uniformly flat that there wasn't a single trapped air bubble in sight, almost as if it had been done using a machine, so efficiently that not a millimetre of wasted tape protruded beyond its smooth edges; the other possibility that occurred to me was that it had been wrapped by the hands of a woman. The former, cold in its systematic invariability, the latter, skilled with delicate precision. If I was seeing no difference between the two, did that mean I was equating the feminine with being mechanistic? I wasn't so sure about that, but what I was certain that my feminist friend would surely tell me off for even thinking that. My feminist friend . . .

Sofia! Of course, how could I forget? I half reproached myself as I struggled with prying open the package.

The duct tape was overly sticky and cumbersome. Of course, the only person who thought the usage of heavy-duty tape was appropriate must have been KenSon, and not any woman.

Finally, I got it open.

Ash fell from my cigarette. I was dumbfounded.

Shrink wrapped in plastic before me was the same stainless-steel, yinyang pot that Mother and I had used to eat mala hot pot in Sanya about a month ago. Why the hell had she sent the pot all the way back to China from Malaysia when I had already made no secret of its uselessness to me?

One by one, I began to remove the contents of the box and placed them on the kitchen table. Apart from the pot, there were several packets of 3-in-1 coffee and Milo, curry powder, Hainanese chicken rice mix, *bak kut teh* mix and instant noodles with the generic red-and-yellow Maggi branding, that always made it seem like staple McDonald's junk food.

I stopped when I got to the pack of red Marlboro cigarettes. Did my mother really send this? Conceivably, she had brought the pot all the way home to Malaysia, only to realize how many pots of far superior quality already existed in her pantry. Thus began its voyage back to China with KenSon, under the pretence that I might need this sorry excuse for a cooking utensil in my life, a receptacle so thin and flimsy it was barely good enough to be a saucepan.

I didn't bother with the rest of items and swept the cache of processed foods into the box once more, jammed it inside the plywood cabinet and shut its doors with a bang.

Then I went back for the pack of Marlboros and lit one.

I smoked my cigarette in silence and solitude, entering into a pleasant withdrawal from the world. Gazing out of the stained windowpane into the streets of Xuhui, I felt happily removed from the crowd of spirits drifting down the cold and windy avenue, in my own peaceful abyss.

All to myself this night was; all to myself the future could be.

There were times when I felt I should jot down these little moments of enlightenment, for snippets of wisdom came rarely for me. But no matter how scarce I was for insight, I never bothered to reach for my pen, for usually the shortcomings of my pithy aphorisms were exposed the following day when the effects of the alcohol subsided, rendering them into nothing but tautological truisms better eradicated than preserved for posterity.

I got up and swung the cabinet open once more, causing fine dust motes to glitter in the half-light of the evening receding before me. With the plastic wrapping crinkling between my fingers, I suddenly remembered an old instant-noodle recipe I simply could not resist cooking up.

Maggi goreng. You didn't have to be hungry to want it.

When I was in Malaysia, someone at a mamak stall once told me that girls who hate instant noodles might make it as classy girlfriends but in reality it's the women who know how to prepare a decent plate of Maggi goreng who cut it as real wife material.

Now people said all kinds of bullshit at the mamak, in this case, mostly sad single men trying to feel better about the sorry state of their own existence. If any generalization, sexist or not, were to endure the test of time, it had to bear at least a semblance of truth, but even so, one would be ill advised to make the jump from its verisimilitude to complete belief without prior verification.

The problem with people is that, people just don't care to verify their opinions at all, I thought, as I diced up half an onion, and then a smaller red onion after that.

So how about if I verified whether I'd make a good househusband?

I decided to take up the challenge. *Cili padi* was the next ingredient I needed to prep, which I had long lamented not being able to get in Shanghai at all. I did, however, have the dried Sichuan variety that would end up completely overpowering the dish, not to mention leaving the tongue numb and oozing with saliva. That simply wouldn't do. I was trying to have a snack, not cripple my palate. I reached inside the fridge and pulled out a milder alternative in my trusty, greasy, not-sure-if-expired bottle of Lao Gan Ma chilli oil, so common in every household in China that people often joked that the signature red label with a portrait of Tao Huabi—godmother of fast meals and late-night snacks—was sacred, omnipresent and omniscient. The recipe also called for a teaspoonful each of ketchup, soy and chilli sauce, none of which I bothered with as they were either condiments I didn't have, or I felt they weren't really worth the effort of rummaging through my pantry for.

The sacred Lao Gan Ma chilli oil of yore would have to work its magic.

I cut open the shrink wrap and gave the noodles a rinse, then on to the gas stove I placed the most-travelled yinyang pot in all of China. Next, I poured water into one half of the bifurcated pot and set it to boil, but quickly realized that my idea of boiling the noodles in one side and frying up the condiments in the other was none too wise. This split cauldron was designed for hot pot, for heating and boiling two kinds of soup evenly, which made half boiling and half stir-frying Maggi goreng less than ideal.

But, having come this far, I couldn't give up already.

I boiled the water in a kettle instead and used it to fill one half of the yinyang pot. Into the other half I added some peanut oil that was just enough to fry everything I had chopped up. In the time that it took for the water to bubble in the yuan and the oil to sizzle in the yang, I racked my brain for the actual procedure of cooking the noodles because, even though I knew what was typically put into the dish, the finer details of the recipe remained hazy to me. For how long should I cook the noodles to ensure it retained a moist and bouncy texture? What ratio of chilli and seasoning to noodle should I use? Should I fry the egg separately or mix it all in?

I didn't think, and just went at it. Such was the art of *agak-agak* cooking, based on rough estimates of ingredients and the arbitrary nature of how the individual feels a dish should be prepared. Even though I was now dealing with simple instant noodles, agak-agak cooking could be used for any dish at all. It was a skill I had developed over the years as an undemanding bachelor and lazy home cook, and I would say I had more successful dishes than failures when using this very approximate method.

As I attempted to fry the instant noodles, however, I wished I had used a normal wok which distributed heat more evenly even if, in the agak-agak world, a bifurcated pot ought to have worked just well . . .

The Maggi goreng didn't end up well, and I wouldn't make the cut as a good househusband.

The Lao Gan Ma tasted just all right—*passable*, as some would say—although it lacked the fresh punch of spice that cili padi packed when one bit into it, and being chilli oil, it lent a greasy, unappealing redness to the finished dish as well. Needless to say, it was not a substitute for fresh chilli, and while on the topic of fresh ingredients, lime or *limau kasturi* was also something I missed dearly, to be squeezed over the fried Maggi noodles, into my iced tea or in the occasional dosage of sweet rose syrup I would drink on humid nights at the wooden shed of a riverside *warung* stall, waiting for the winds to carry away the torrid heat and stench hovering just above the muddy banks.

I ate about half of it, binned the rest and lit another Marlboro.

Was I lonelier back then than I was now? I wasn't able to say for sure. The palms and coconuts I used to watch, rustling with the river breeze like petrified bodies swaying in unison, were now replaced by stoic buildings that didn't. Everything existed under that eternal smog engulfing every light of the city like a false ceiling, where at times there was scarcely any difference between day and night, not a shred of light between bitterness and empathy.

Wasn't that what being Chinese was all about? A wilful eating of bitterness through thick and thin, all the while facing the capriciousness and turbulence of the changing times, in a world claiming to be in the middle of everything that exists?

After moving to China, I realized that 21st-century Chinese society certainly wasn't what I had presumed it would be, especially when compared with the 'overseas Chinese' community in Malaysia which I found to be generally more adherent to the supposed tenets and traditional values of the Zhonghua minzu.

Were we Malaysian Chinese part of the Zhonghua minzu? Did I wish to be embroiled in such a politically loaded term?

I could still hear my mother making the impassioned proclamation in the back seat of that van which we had hired in Hainan, that this idea of an all-encompassing Zhonghua minzu race had formed so great a bond among its peoples that it transcended not only the newly erected borders following Malaya's independence, but also our own version of patriotism and allegiance to a post-colonial statehood still in its infancy. I understood that, for some people, clinging to an ethnic identity originating from a country far more advanced in their respective social, economic and military infrastructures was that much easier than to continue the struggle in an underdeveloped, post-colonial land that left much more to be desired of its government and citizens.

But what about me? Was I able to verify that statement? Did I see myself more as a Malaysian or more as a Han Chinese belonging to the Zhonghua minzu?

I stubbed out the cigarette.

I despised nationalism and the whole idea of a unitary identity; the very thought of it filled me with intense disgust. The topic had the effect of putting my mind through a heavy-duty wash cycle, first in surreptitious whirls before the many steady rounds of spinning, all to wring my consciousness free of dirt at the expense of ripping its seams.

If real life meant the necessity of participating in the political, then I didn't want real life to matter for me. Not when actual life was right here for anyone's taking, be it for the Han Manchu Meng or Hui in China, or the Chinese Malay Indian or Orang Asli in Malaysia. After all, it was all in the name of colonialism that our forefathers were indentured, toiling away and tilling the earth for tin in the early 19th century, stopping only to smoke cheap tobacco, to spit and momentarily shake off the soil sticking beneath their feet.

In the name of work, they must've known that bitterness was a common wound necessary to life, for what other force could propel one in search of the taste of sweetness upon the tips of their tongues time after time, again and again?

Chapter 16

I came to the conclusion late one night, as I braced myself for warmth in the face of the biting north winds, that the ultimate decluttering possible in life was only attainable through a state of worklessness. The idea wasn't quite Leo Tolstoy renouncing his wealth to pursue a life of asceticism. In my life was no Konstantin Dmitrievich Levin to take pity on me as an overworked peasant on his estate, and there certainly was no Stepan Oblonsky proposing for him to give me that estate. I just felt that it was time to leave the peasant's hut. So, after the turn of the year, I decided to stop going in to the *TRIESTE* office and quit my job with immediate effect.

In the following weeks, I was confronted with mindless amounts of free time I simply didn't know how to utilize; in part, because I wasn't desperate to fill it with anything meaningful. Even with all the time, I still didn't cook my own food, and found myself either going out to eat at the same restaurants or getting the same Waimai orders from the takeaways I liked. From afternoon to evening, I would go out to sit and hang out at the same bars and cafés with a copy of *War and Peace* that I really struggled with and burned far too many cigarettes reading. I gave up after my fourth trip to the *yanjiudian* and exchanged the book with the scholarly shopkeeper for a pack of Liqun and a cold beer.

I was expecting some kind of divine change to come over my life but, after a few weeks of having all this extra free time, the only noticeable difference was a single digit wiped off my bank account balance.

With each passing day, I found myself sleeping in much later and waking up whenever I felt like it. One night, as I was rummaging in KenSon's parcel for a midnight snack of instant noodles, right at the bottom of the pile of instant noodles and *bak kut teh* mix I found a journal and a beautiful fountain pen in aquamarine colour which I had somehow overlooked before. I stubbed out my cigarette and let the heft of the polished-steel pen rest in between my fingers.

In my following afternoons at the café, I started to handwrite poems and short verse without direction, freely exploring the rhythms and types of prose that were shut off to me when I was writing for *TRIESTE*; digging deep in the hope of finding a unique style that I could call my own. As someone who hadn't written on paper since university, my handwriting was utterly inexcusable. *That looks really shit*, I could hear KenSon's voice go in my head. *Thanks to this gift from an asshole, I shall now become a poet*, I wrote.

I wrote, ate and slept. The fleeting hours of daylight somehow made the days feel even longer.

Every night, I would lie in bed on the threshold of sleeplessness. Where once were vast empty plains now stood high walls, and in place of the strolls I took under a nebulous sky into dreams, now loomed the towering task of entering the impenetrable realm of unconsciousness.

A drink of water. A smoke. A half sentence written down.

Eventually I would always return to a place where the way to rest remained shut to me. Every night, I longed for the darkness to engulf me, and to carry me further into a space where rest was promised. Willingly, I lay prone and vulnerable to the vicissitudes of the night with my eyes closed, hoping for rest.

It was during the small hours that I felt the second night open and unfold before me.

There, as I lay restless, came the sound of footsteps from outside my window. I could just about make out a whirring noise that sounded more eerie the longer it went on, always followed by two short clicks. I got up and drifted towards the amber world outside my window. How had sleep come to be so far removed from me?

By the sidewalk was a silhouette, as female as shadows go. I watched her as she began to set down a tripod, which she clicked into place with every extension of its slender limbs. Deliberately, the shadow manipulated a silver camera on top of the tripod, angling it until she was satisfied with the framing of the shot. She then pulled out a device from her pocket and pointed it in the direction of the scene several times before firing the camera with a button connected via a rubber tube. Her every movement appeared purposeful, her every manipulation of the camera methodical.

What on earth was there to shoot on the streets of Xuhui? At this hour? In the cold of winter? Merry drunks? A documentation of the homeless? Old French buildings shrouded in tenebrosity?

I might as well find out, I thought. So, I threw on the thickest parka I could find, and descended the stairs into the cold.

'Are you here to take my picture?' I called out from behind the very feminine shadow, inadvertently startling her which in turn startled me.

'Sorry, I tried my best not to creep, but ended up doing so anyway . . .'

'I've been looking for you, so that's all right. It was the night that led me here.'

I felt the gaze of the shadow suffuse me, wholly bestowing me with a welcomed sense of familiarity and I was able to look back at her as I used to, watching her exhale puff after puff of cigarette smoke before finally flicking the butt towards the ground.

This was how I came to be reunited with the girl named Sofia. Was it out of a necessity concerning fate, or perhaps even an ill twist of it, I didn't know. What was clear was that she no longer went by the name Sofia, and no longer did she seem like the spontaneous girl who went for jianbing and crab noodles on a whim, no longer the nymphet I had almost slept with and never expected to cross paths with ever again. This time around, she had come to me in the form of a shadow, a shadow that now went by her real name of Gao Yuan Fei. I obliged myself to call her nothing else.

Yuan Fei resumed her position behind the worn, silver camera mounted on the tripod, which under the fading paint one could make out a beautiful, brass patina. She continued to measure the surrounding area with her light meter, while I unabashedly helped myself to a cigarette from the pack she had left on the bench since I had left mine upstairs. I lit up, and before I even realized that a bus was passing by from behind me, Yuan Fei had already turned the tripod towards me and fired the shutter with her rubber cable release. A long *whirrrrrr* ensued before the shutter closed with a click.

'Can I see?'

'No.'

'Come on, show me.'

'It's a film camera.'

'You're no fun at all.'

Yuan Fei picked up the pack of cigarettes and crushed it. I had loutishly taken the last one from her, and it seemed like I was about to pay the ultimate price.

'You actually took my last cigarette?'

'Don't get mad. I have more upstairs if you want.'

'No, no . . . I'm done with you. Shanghai is big enough to afford me other men. I need to get back to shooting.'

'For heaven's sake, I'm not asking you to come upstairs . . . just hold on while I get you the cigarettes.'

I rushed through the doors and up the stairs, my heart racing.

When I got back, Yuan Fei had already packed up her tripod, but let me stay on to watch her shoot the shikumen-style houses of the French Concession. We began to walk in no particular direction as she shot more photographs. She told me she was shooting a silver Leica M3 from 1955 with a pre-aspherical Summilux 35mm lens, and the film she used was called Kodak Tri-X, which she preferred over Ilford HP5. These were both 400 ISO films, but Tri-X had a finer grain and better contrast ratios ideal for her work, Ilford HP5 was a little too gritty for her. She also told me about the aperture and focal length of the lens, something about the diminishing returns in aperture value of the Summiluxes compared to Summicron lens. Then she said she idolized Daido Moriyama, although she wasn't that fond of digital and she didn't have the proficiency of shooting a 28mm wide angle lens, saying she had trouble getting that close and directly in the face of her subjects. I just nodded every now and again as though I understood, following closely behind her.

Unlike the well-worn camera she clutched against her chest, her black, avant-garde coat looked to be fresh off the rack of a designer showroom in Xintiandi and as it billowed against the midnight wind with its long hem barely clearing the ground, she seemed to glide forward with every stride, no longer as a shadow but a grim reaper running on nicotine. 'So, what do you do now? Still writing editorials for that media page?'

I thought better of telling her about the poetry. For now, it was something personal between me and farm boy, Tony Leung.

'Well, I'm just a traveller without employment at this point.'

'What? What about your visa?' she asked, lowering the viewfinder from her eyes.

'I don't know. I'll need to check my passport.'

'Well, that just won't do. Why don't you come work for me?'

'For you?'

'Right, for me. You write good English.'

'Of course, but what would you need me to write?'

'We'll discuss that later. Let me finish this roll and we'll talk about it over supper.'

Supper? Just one more roll?

By the time she was finally finished, we were having breakfast at a *doujiang* store that was only just opening for the day.

'Fun night out? I'll bring you some hot tea to sober up,' said the store owner uncle who was dressed in nothing but a grimy singlet in the cold of winter.

'We're great, uncle, actually perfectly sober,' Yuan Fei smiled. 'Could you bring us some hot soymilk?'

'Sober, huh? Kids these days don't do it right . . .'

'Kid? *Shushu*, I'm almost thirty.'

'You're kidding? Thirty . . . the age of independence! Well, I must say, those are some youthful genes you have, or perhaps I should consider staying out later,' he laughed.

'You're thirty?'

'More or less so. Why . . . does it matter to you now?'

She lit up another cigarette. Behind her, chief doujiang sheepishly raised an eyebrow.

Ahem, I cleared my throat, accepting the ashtray the chief brought over.

'What were we talking about, again?'

'Let's see,' she said, her mouth full of smoke, 'you're going to come work for me. I'll pay you well, and you won't have to worry about your visa. I'll handle it.'

'What would you have me do?'

'I'm entrusting you with the task of writing my biography.'

'A biography? Like your life story?'

'More like an artist's log I'm supposed to keep.'

'Why can't you do it?'

'Because I think you can do it better. Plus, it'll free up the time for me to work more on photography.'

I thought about it for a while, staring into space. This was too much out of the blue, and I had been sleepless for days.

'You don't have to give me an answer right now; take some time to think about it. Unless my age has suddenly put you off?'

'Lai lai! Hot food incoming!' interrupted the chief as he scurried over as if sensing danger in my indecision. 'Here's your salty doujiang and youtiao for you! Don't burn your throat, it's awfully hot!'

We dug in. The doujiang was not only awfully hot, but awfully salty too. I was immediately overcome with thirst and in my state of insomnia, I stupidly attempted to quench it by drinking several more mouthfuls of the hearty broth. Doujiang with seaweed, vinegar and soy sauce topped with scallions and crispy, deep-fried youtiao. You couldn't get anything like it in Malaysia, especially with the general public preferring to load up on sugar not sodium, or anything vaguely considered healthy for that matter.

She motioned for the bill; I drained what was left in my bowl.

'Please do come again, young people,' said the chief, as he watched us step outside to go across the street for Yuan Fei's customary, post-meal cigarette. From under a leafless sycamore tree, we stood watching the breakfast crowd slowly trickle into the doujiang store.

'So, what say you?'

'You can't expect me to answer now.'

'Why not? You swamped with work or something?'

In my sleep-deprived state it felt like every drag I took went straight to my head, clouding it so much that I could only spew smoke in the place of words.

I hadn't seen her for half a year and at that I had only ever met her twice. How was I to answer? I guess I was in need of a job, but then again, I was approaching a point where I didn't care whether I stayed in China or got deported back to Malaysia. To stay or not to stay, posed itself as a non-question to me. I'd had the experience of being jobless in Malaysia before, but I found this state of unemployment in China to be quite surreal for me. With each passing day, I existed merely and purely for myself, and even the simple act of watching people go about their daily grind from my bedroom window would bring me a deep sense of peace. In my current state of existence in the world's largest capitalist state, I was able to see and understand that I was both foreign and Chinese, simultaneously dedicated and lazy to the bone, that I was someone born without a dream, almost hopeful that life would turn the very next corner.

'I just need to ask, who's going to be reading your biography if I write it?'

'Are you the police? Always full of questions and no answers.'

'Okay, I'll rephrase: why does it need writing in the first place? What's the profile for?'

'I'm working on an exhibition, hopefully for the Museum of Photography in Berlin. I'll be putting together a series of prints in monochrome, and I think it'll be nice if someone could document the whole process. A good profile would really help establish myself as a photographer.'

'Ah! That's . . . amazing. That's in Germany, right? What's the series going to be about?'

Yuan Fei smiled and finished smoking her cigarette. I could tell she wasn't ready to divulge that information.

'At least tell me the working title. If I'm to write your biography, you need to get me curious too.'

'It's called Unquiet Heart Soliloquy.'

'Unquiet Heart . . . Soliloquy?'

'Yes. That's it.'

Chapter 17

Gao Yuan Fei is a thirty-one-year-old photographer from Hangzhou, capital city of Zhejiang province in China. The style of her work teeters on the border of hyper realism and the everyday, and she is not shy to point to the underlying Dionysian traits shown by her subjects within the frame. Gao believes that a photograph in itself offers no narrative context to its viewer whatsoever. Instead, what an image captured by the camera opens is a space for the viewer to step into, much like an intrusion, a colonization of the image by the mind. With this, photography has no subject, it is the individual viewer who shapes and moulds a context within the frame, displacing form and constructing a unique kind of plasticity with their own eyes. If there is to be a subject in photography, Gao believes that it should be the individual peering in from outside of the frame. There can be no God behind the viewfinder.

Gao tells me she is sponsored by the local Crescent Moon (Xinyue) Dealership. That reminds me of the Crescent Moon Society established by Xu Zhimo, I remark. But Gao says she isn't a fan of new-school, modern Chinese poetry with its stringent usage of syllables and metrics. But aren't you trying to be modern with photography? I ask.

Well, anyone can try, but not many succeed, she replies.

Gao is particularly fond of the poetry of Xi Chuan and the films of Lou Ye. Great artists working under censorship, I remark.

She smiles, something she doesn't do very often when working. Artists cannot be concerned about censorship, she shrugs.

Gao develops and scans her work at her home studio on the outskirts of Hangzhou by the West Lake. She shoots extensively with her arsenal of film cameras, the Leica M3 being her main one, and among many others also a Mamiya 6 square medium format camera and a Minolta TC-1 point and shoot. She also shoots digital on occasion, although surprisingly she shuns DSLRs and APS-C cameras, preferring the more disruptive iPhones to document the more mundane moments in her life. A picture of her shoes after a night out, a snapshot of the dishes washed and stacked up neatly by the sink, the way her hair looks differently every time she dries it with a towel.

It might seem odd that, being someone who is around cameras and who uses them so much, Gao doesn't consider everything she does with a camera as photography. She started shooting in her preparation for postgraduate studies in architecture, as she sought to document a kind of 'self-gentrification' phenomenon she observed in Chinese cities, where occupants would experience a drastic and very sudden increase in wealth due to pay-outs given by the government in order to possess their homes for redevelopment. But soon after shooting a handful of sites, she gave up on submitting the application to university.

'I didn't feel like what I had to say about gentrification was in any way significant to the lives of the people living in these buildings,' she tells me.

Once she accomplished her architectural research goal of photographing homes, by shooting 100 rolls of black-and-white film—almost exclusively Kodak Tri-X and Shanghai GP3— she experienced major burnout and became disillusioned in the project virtually overnight.

'I just left the film undeveloped for the longest time, two big plastic bags lying in a corner of my apartment in Shanghai.

At first, I couldn't even bear looking at the bags, because the thought of failure was just so overwhelming. After some time . . . I began to see them as nothing more than a peculiar decoration for my room.'

Everything changed when she eventually developed them, almost a full year later.

Gao then began to see things in a new light.

'I was, of course, still photographing during the course of the year, either just for fun or as an experiment for pulling and pushing film. But when I finally sat down with the scans from my failed university application, I suddenly gained a better idea of what I had been trying to do all this time, which was not so much to research, but to document the real lives of people. So many ideas started to flow my way, as if the sluice gates had just been opened in a dry canal. I decided to shelve my pursuit of architecture for the time being. I knew I had to continue shooting photographs.'

Yuan Fei lowered my journal and placed it on the coffee table. I set the glass of *Longjingcha* I had been sipping down on the rattan mat, eager to hear what she thought. But had she finished the entire article? No one was that fast a reader.

Through the tall, glass-window walls on the other side of us was the West Lake in winter, where, on the fringes, beyond the sparse lotus hanging their heads in solemn dormancy, no peach or plum-blossom tree was left unbleached by snow. The scene was like a Wang Wei poem, I wanted to tell her, but then it felt like such a general and completely ordinary remark. Not a Tang poem but a Wang Wei poem, I felt only she would understand that. I waited and waited, but in her Barcelona chair across from me, she remained a picture of stoicism.

'It's good. But I can't read any more,' she said.

'What do you mean?'

'Keep writing, but don't show it to me.'

'What about the editing? Or the direction of the writing?'

Yuan Fei looked out at the lake and took in a deep breath, then she dragged on her cigarette, the resulting trail of smoke resembling a discharge more than an exhalation. A sigh. The sight of the tranquil lake with its undisturbed waters was infinitely calming. If I squinted really hard, I could just about make out the daily fanfare of multi-storeyed tourist boats all the way on the east bank.

'I just can't stand reading about myself, seeing my name in the flux of narration . . . I've seen enough to trust you with this project,' she replied, pausing for a sip of tea, after which she tucked a loose fringe behind her ear with a sweep of her hand. 'An artist doesn't do art to confront the self, but to escape from it. Don't write that down, okay? Now let's eat.'

That was my cue to start prepping the day's lunch. It was almost 1 p.m. This was much later than Yuan Fei usually ate and just about the time I would start thinking how I should avoid starving myself. In a strange twist of fate, ever since I moved to Hangzhou, over the past two months, I found myself taking up the duties of cooking. Yuan Fei didn't have to ask me, it was just one of those things that naturally fell into place simply because she was working most of the time, and it wasn't as though I had much to occupy myself with when I wasn't writing.

Fortunately, I had wrapped a whole lot of dumplings earlier this morning that wouldn't take too long to boil and serve. Pork-and-chive dumplings was one of those dishes that had seemed really complicated to me at first, but soon became second nature to me after a few botched attempts. The recipe called for a holy trinity of ingredients: pork with a good fat content, garlic chives and dumpling wrappers. After mincing the pork and chopping the chives, I incorporated them with sesame oil, soy sauce, dark soy sauce, salt and bit of sugar—an egg is optional if one uses more chives to pork for better binding of proteins—before wrapping them in robust dumpling wrappers that retained a good bite to them but also a silky smooth texture on the outside when boiled. I guess, after breaking it down and getting into the nitty-gritty of the recipe, it's not so much a holy trinity at all, but just minced pork and chives mixed with everything one can find in a Chinese pantry, wrapped in dough, then dunked in boiling water. Above all it was crucial to start early so that I could give myself sufficient preparation time, as there was a tendency in me to become quite preoccupied with my morning writing and let the morning get away from me. Now, after all the hard work had been done, dumping the jiaozi into the bubbling wok felt so gratifying that the misery of waking up early to chop up a thawed, yet frigid, piece of pork shoulder, then whisking it together with a raw egg and chives until incorporated into a sticky paste (using chopsticks of course), followed by the finger-numbing kneading of dumpling wrappers from scratch, using nothing but hot water and flour on a late winter's marble table top, dissipated entirely.

I scooped up the dumplings and allowed the water to drain through the sieve. All I had to do now was plate them and try not to burn the black vinegar dipping sauce in the wok.

Yuan Fei was famished. It was not the hour nor the way in which she consumed her share of dumplings that betrayed this, but the resounding silence permeating the lakeside dining room as we ate.

'It needs cornflour, for bite and a firmer texture,' she pointed out astutely.

'We've run out. All used up on the gongbao chicken.'

'Hardly surprising—that dish was way too gunky. You added too much. In fact, I don't think gongbao chicken needs cornflour at all.'

'Really? But then it'll be too dry and without a glaze.'

'It's all about timing, and cooking chicken on the bone helps to preserve moisture.'

I wasn't really sure where she was going with this. I didn't think it would taste good—a plate of dry chicken with an unthickened, watery sauce. Or was she not planning on having a sauce at all? I said I would give it a try sometime . . . and left it at that.

Yuan Fei and I were taking our first winter together one day at a time. We worked daily but struggled to sustain any extended period of productivity beyond the ebb and flow of creative spurts that came. Even if we were completely focused and barely talked for hours, with her staring hard at and annotating a contact sheet, and me documenting her process of staring at and annotating a contact sheet—we were rarely satisfied with our work, and it was difficult to pinpoint the reason for this.

After lunch Yuan Fei went back to work in her studio. The workspace was minimalistic and modestly sized with tall ceilings and high, glass windows, furnished with a long, rectangular standing desk, a bookshelf, a few lateral-filing cabinets and a large beanbag. Fluorescent lights, encased in smooth aluminium, hung from the ceiling in two parallel rows. With no proper sitting furniture, one got the sense that it was very much a workspace where she would come in to get things done and leave. An abundance of natural light filled the studio no matter the time of day or season. Yuan Fei kept the room exceptionally tidy, and at times I would sneak inside by myself just to soak in the meditative atmosphere bestowed by its sheer emptiness. I'm sure Wittgenstein would approve.

Adjoined via a corridor to the studio, was a modern, one-storey house where we each had our own room. I worked in a reading room filled with 1930s Art Deco Chinese furniture, an eclectic second living room within the house, where I spent many hours staring at the blinking cursor on my screen as it grew more hypnotic by the day. At times, when I got up from the Ming calligraphy desk to brew coffee—which Yuan Fei had been surprisingly blasé about my using since the day I moved in—I would often question not only my role as Yuan Fei's biographer, but also my purpose of being in China. I found it increasingly difficult to write and attributed my declining output to my increasingly lackadaisical attitude towards gainful employment. On some days I wrote, but on most days I didn't. Through the vines of the garden willow, I watched the days drift by with the quiet currents of the lake, until one day spring arrived and roused me from the poignancy of winter. Only then did it dawn on me, one day as I walked past the eclectic reading room which Yuan Fei had, over the years, put together with the help of a Shanghai dealer, that she had been using it less and less, to the point where she no longer came in for her customary pot of tea and two cigarettes there around 4 p.m. every day.

Had I become an intruder in her home? A nuisance that never ceased playing at the back of her head?

This didn't happen to be a question which I was prepared to simply ask her, not when she was always busy at work in the next room—either totally submerged in drafting and editing the next series of prints or being fixated by a new batch of contact sheets back from the lab. If I wanted to talk, I had to pick my moment, mid-morning was usually the best time, right after she had completed a thorough once-over of the previous day's work, putting her in an upbeat and more receptive mood.

However, when I entered the studio late the next morning, Yuan Fei was nowhere to be found. I walked over to stand in front of the tall windows and bathed in the sunlight it afforded, only lamenting the fact that I was not able to peer outside from its apex. What a view that would be! I turned around. The minimalistic room looked even more bare in her absence, and the advent of springtime chiming in from outside only accentuated the sense of calm emptiness, which no doubt incited tendencies for reflection in any artist. But wasn't the converse also true, that reflection itself also made the self feel empty?

I hadn't eaten breakfast, so I left my pseudo-intellectual, philosophical musings in the studio, put on my beat-up Air Maxes and trotted out through the arched-moon gate to get my fix of shengjianbao and piping-hot, soy milk. It felt like the longest time since I last had a pan-fried baozi, so toothsome in its every morsel, and even longer still since I had left the house. I had yet to explore Hangzhou and knew next to nothing about it except for its production of strong Liqun cigarettes, although it still surprised me that I couldn't find a single baozi shop on the promenade fronting the West Lake, where the throngs of early spring tourists milled about, full of mirth.

I quickly turned away from the touristy street and after a brisk fifteen-minute walk that was barely even the Chinese pedestrian shed, I stepped into the first noodle house I chanced upon, a *pianerchuan* noodle shop that I later discovered was a Hangzhou delicacy dating back to the mid-19th century. Only a quarter of the store's seating was occupied, so I managed to find a seat and order with ease and in no time, I was wolfing down a hearty bowl of hand-pulled noodles, pausing only to blow away the steam rising off the top of the snow-white cabbage, green bamboo shoots and red lean pork.

I polished it off in no time and ordered another. This time, only as I waited did I notice the plaque on the wall that read: *yǒu sǔn yǒu ròu bù shòu bù sú xuě cài shāo miàn shénxiān kǒufú*, which translates roughly into with bamboo and pork we are neither thin nor bad, snow cabbage hot noodles even gods' mouths water.

'You've settled in nicely, seeing that you found such a local place to eat.'

Hearing a familiar voice made me turn around, for a moment wishfully thinking it was Luna whom I had failed so miserably to meet since coming here. For better or worse, Shanghai and Hangzhou were now cities that defined a greater part of my late twenties, whether its narrative was about moving abroad to confront the fickle undulations at play within one's heart, or the importance of hard work to overcome the emotions that threatened to explode within me. The pain I felt had to be mitigated somehow, and a lot of it was down to Gao Yuan Fei, who was standing behind me looking bemused at the way I was looking at her.

She put down her shopping bags and took the seat across from me.

'Another bowl of noodles over here!' she hollered.

'Already on it!' came the reply.

'What's up with you?' she asked with a smile. She seemed very surprised that I had made it out of the house.

'Nothing. Just very hungry, that's all.'

'Well, you've come to a good place; this is a third-generation, noodle business,' she said as she poured tea for both of us and gave a nod to the proprietor as he brought over two bowls of noodles. I blew on mine and started slurping, this time with slightly more decorum.

Her eyes widened. I probably ought to have waited for her.

'Oh yes, I got you something this morning,' she said, rummaging through her haul for a rectangular box which she then handed over to me. 'For your first spring in China.'

I opened the box to reveal a pair of crossed-strapped Velcro sandals—black, of course, as most of Yuan Fei's effects were—with the word *SUICOKE* subtly stitched on to the square, fabric label. They were so sturdy and well made. At the very centre of its underside was the famed Vibram outsole with a rubber-etched logo. Even in my coarse, unwitting hands I was able to appreciate how delicately constructed an item it was. I don't think I had ever owned anything this nice.

'You shouldn't have.'

'I've just about lost patience with those dirty Air Maxes, so don't mention it. Plus, I just got paid.'

'No, I mean, you shouldn't have gotten a black pair; the dark colour detracts from the beauty of the silhouette, and you can't see any details. Quite literally, it overshadows the unique shape of the sandal.'

'No way! If anything, black accentuates the pure and simple silhouette of the sandal. Why would you want to see the details on a sandal anyway? Footwear should be worn for comfort, not to make a statement.'

'Who cares about making a statement? Imagine . . . sand or olive straps would look so much better strapped around my bare feet in spring. Think dark chinos or khaki shorts, super casual! Maybe even with socks to go with a pair of washed or raw-selvedge denim with the cuffs folded up.'

'Sandals with socks . . .? Can't figure if that's more bourgeois or bohemian. Anyway, do you want to swap it for another colour? Something more complementary to your skin tone perhaps?'

'That's hardly necessary when everything complements yellow,' I laughed. 'Now, how about we do the noodles justice before it turns cold?'

When we stepped outside the noodle shop, the late morning sun was dazzlingly bright. I hadn't realized how much I had missed its warmth during the long winter and was momentarily enthralled by the warmth of the rays that caressed my skin, something I took completely for granted in Malaysia. It was so nice out that we ended up wandering for a bit before heading back to the studio. We tried to avoid the stretch of the lakeside promenade for the most part but, even through the less crowded streets off from the main, there was still no way of steering completely clear of the herd of parents on a day out with their children, the groups of university students on dates in this fashionable part of the city, or the sheer flux of tourists both foreign and local.

We walked without talking. Oddly enough, with neither of us sheepishly flicking away cigarette butts, because neither of us was smoking. Yuan Fei looked beautiful, even more so than the time I knew her simply as Sofia, the architecture student, even as she squinted against the glare of the midday sun, or when she stopped to curse the pollen for triggering a violent sneeze.

The cadence of our walk was interrupted when she gradually slowed, until stopping dead in her tracks right by the crossing on the other side of the Zhejiang Art Museum, looking on wistfully at a group of workers taking down the large banners for a contemporary photo exhibition hanging down the left and right façade of the building. A steady stream of pedestrians passed by us as the crosswalk lights turned from red to green and back again. The distant look of yearning on her face was not one that I could immediately comprehend. All I could offer then was a hand on her shoulder. She turned and walked away.

'Should we have a stroll across the Su Causeway? I don't think you've seen it,' she asked after gathering herself.

'Isn't that all the way across to the west? And then all the way across the lake to the north?'

'Yes.'

'And a really long walk?'

'You're not wrong.'

'Well, okay then, feels like months since I've had a good walk. Do you want to get some cigarettes first?'

'I've quit smoking. It's too tedious.'

'You mean it feels too much like work?'

'Perhaps. But in my case, it feels more like an eternal thorn in my side.'

'Care to elaborate?'

'Well, Nietzsche's theory of eternal return may not be all that plausible . . . but just imagine if what he's postulating were true! I wouldn't want to spend my lifetimes sneaking away for a smoke every half hour ad infinitum. There's got to be better things to do after coming back as recycled matter, lifetime after lifetime.'

In the distance ahead we could see the long stretch of the Su Causeway, its green embankments split every few hundred metres by stone bridges.

I asked her more about the theory and took a moment to mull over what she said, allowing my mind to really chew on it. The lake beside us was an opaque cyan colour, forming murky reflections of the lakeside greenery and the sun now at its highest point in the sky. It wasn't all that hot out, but I already felt the perspiration forming under my shirt. Eternal return? It sounded like a good name for a middle-class, retirement scheme.

'But aren't you already saying that as an amalgam of recycled matter? Who knows what kind of being those carbon and oxygen molecules may have made up in your past life, or how many cycles they have gone through before.'

'Perhaps I am, but there's more to it than that. Because I'm not merely talking about matter in this case, but also the metaphysical configurations given through biochemical matter that makes up the self. There's a metaphysical makeup for the self that wants to quit smoking; the self who wants to still smoke when there's nothing but a dead end in her work; the self who wants to travel even though she'll feel lonely wherever she is in the world; the self who is not afraid to be feminine even in an Internet age where feminism has utterly failed to live up to the spirit of radicalism it exhibited in the '50s and '60s.'

'Do you believe there's a true self in every one of us? Something unique in every person?'

'That's one of the worst things in the world you can do: to feel that your selfhood is unique. Do we have free will? Perhaps so, as I'm willing myself not to smoke today. Do human beings meander and find ways through life by abiding to a higher unknowable moral code in accordance with our humanity? I say maybe, maybe not. For example, smoking has nothing to do with morals, unless you're constantly exhaling in another's face and feeding your cigarette butts to the mallards. To say that there's a true self within each individual—in this fickle new millennium where we split hairs over what to eat for lunch, where consumers buy ten variations of the same product on Taobao just to feel something, where we travel not to see with our own eyes but for the benefit of others online—is really quite absurd. Is my true self a self-conscious prude? Or does she not care about the consequences and judgement of others and light up as she desires? I cannot say. The true self fluctuates whenever we try to define it. It is forever on the borders of the personas we inhabit.'

'Okay, I get it. So, there's a Yuan Fei who stays in to work in the confinements of her studio all day, who takes breaks only to cook and water her plants, and on the other hand there's Sofia, who is more outgoing and enjoys spontaneous long walks around the West Lake, across the Su Di and back?'

'You're getting the gist of it, except . . . there's no Sofia any more, just a few different versions of Gao Yuan Fei. Who needs a white person's name anyway?'

'So why did you choose to use that name in the first place?'

'I was young at the time. As an architecture student at Tongji University, everyone wants to stand out and fight for local, then international, recognition. I thought my portfolio would stand out more with an Anglo-Saxon name, I didn't stop to think that it happened to be so generic.'

'And so you went ahead and decided you'd be from Germany.'

'What do you mean?'

'I'm referring to your Tinder profile, of course! You also said you were studying Mandarin in China.'

'Ah! Did it say I was from Germany? I've forgotten all about that,' she laughed. 'I wrote that thing years ago. Once again, at that time I wanted to appeal more to foreigners.'

'You also said you were twenty-four, now that's just like writing fiction at this point.'

'Interested in seeing the Xihu from inside of it, are you? Don't cross the line!'

We laughed and ambled on, passing the rebuilt Leifeng Pagoda on sunset hill which was swarming with tourist vans, hopefully none harbouring anyone aiming to steal the infamous medicinal bricks that caused its collapse in the first place. Only after another fifteen minutes of walking did we reach the edge of the embankment where we crossed the first stone bridge of the Su Causeway to join the crowd of leisurely strolling day trippers and cyclists whizzing by on postman bicycles.

'I like Yuan Fei a lot better,' I said, turning to her.

'Ah . . .?'

'I mean, compared to Sofia Gao from Germany.'

'Well, thanks. It turns out the buyers do as well. With the new wave of orientalism feeding the fine art and photography market, artists with exotic Asian names tend to sell really well.'

'And hopefully you'll be showing in Germany soon.'

'Let's not count on that just yet, my sponsor wants me to show in some local galleries first.'

'Is that the collector you told me about?'

'Yes. It's actually a company based in Wenzhou with which I got acquainted online, although I've only met one of their representatives in person.'

Wenzhou? I immediately thought of Luna, but quickly pushed her out of my mind.

'That sounds convenient. So how does it work?'

'Basically, I sign up with them and they provide me with an allowance for food and film supplies each month, plus they let me stay at the house and use the studio for free.'

'Ah, so that's the deal. I always thought it was your house!'

'My house? Do you know how much it costs to rent something by the West Lake? This one belongs to the chief lady boss, the spirited philanthropist supporting the arts. I, on the other hand, have been saving up.'

'For a house by the West Lake?' I asked, she rolled her eyes.

'For a trip to Europe! My dream is to drive across Germany on the Autobahn, to see, experience and be part the art scene in Berlin; then, perhaps, stop by Dessau to visit some of my friends who are studying to be proper architects at the DIA. After that, I'll continue on to Dresden, to see with my own eyes the baroque architecture rebuilt after World War II; then there's, of course, the Bauhaus Museum in Weimar . . . and of course, I'll want to be photographing every bit of it along the way as well . . .'

Yuan Fei's eyes lit up as she spoke, this was a world within her that was far beyond me.

'But do you know what my absolute goal in Germany is? Apart from the exhibition that is . . .?'

'I don't know. To eat schnitzel in Lederhosen and drink yourself silly?'

'No . . . foreigners don't come to China only to ascend the Great Wall and eat xiaolongbao, do they?'

'Don't most of them do that?'

'Well, I'm not doing the equivalent in Germany! My dream is to go to the Nürburgring circuit, not to do any hot laps but just to keep it on the track during Touristenfahrten. I want to savour the burnt rubber and smell of the asphalt, and perhaps photograph the vulgar graffiti if I can.'

'Wow . . . five minutes ago I didn't even know you drove!'

'Actually, I drive a stick,' she laughed, 'but that's mainly when I'm back home; there's no need for a car here.'

'Wait, aren't you from Hangzhou? This is a lot of new information; I might be getting your biography all wrong.'

'Hangzhou is fine. I'm actually from the outskirts. The buyers won't know it, even many people in China don't know it, so I wouldn't expect you to know it.'

'But what if I want to know it?'

'Don't you worry. Soon you'll know everything . . . in good time,' she smiled.

Chapter 18

I woke in a deep haze. Was the soft light over the West Lake horizon from a new dawn or a fading dusk? I couldn't tell through half-open and misty eyes. Still very lightheaded, I gingerly brought myself to sit upright on the curved Art Deco couch that always made me lie down like a banana.

Ah yes, yes . . .

We had made it halfway across the West Lake before turning back. I was tired, although Yuan Fei insisted that we kept going until we reached the other side. The compromise? We had to take a slight detour for coffee and jianbing along the way home, a teatime guilty pleasure of hers which I quite liked myself.

Upon returning, I remember Yuan Fei washing her face and immediately vanishing into the studio, and I being as industrious as I was, made straight for the curved couch in the reading room to catch a late-afternoon siesta. The box containing the new pair of sandals she had gifted me was exactly where I had left it, on the coffee table by an ashtray full of half-smoked cigarette butts. Were these her final few sticks? If she was quitting tomorrow, I guess she was allowed to smoke today, provided it was still evening. I picked up the ashtray and left the room.

Finding my way down the unlit corridor was difficult and a bit unsettling. It was dark and all too quiet. Something seemed to hang in the air, a presence so strong I felt its furtive movements behind my ears, amplified all the more by the dryness at the back of my throat. The pungent smell of burnt cigarettes assaulting my nostrils seemed to fade. I came to a halt, for how long I cannot ascertain, although, in those suspended moments, many things became clear to me. What hung in the air was silence, a purity given not through the absence of sound, nor by inner tranquillity, but by stepping outside the borders of my unquiet subjectivity. It began to envelop me, not as a sinister force rearing its head, but a friend seeking the warm embrace of a companion. Where have you been? How far have I come since my first steps on this road?

I crept on and left the silence behind at some point because, upon entering the kitchen, I could just about make out someone taking a phone call in the living room. I binned the fag ends and let the tap run over the ashtray before stowing it out of sight. On the kitchen countertop stood a tall glass of Longjingcha filled to the brim.

The kitchen door slid open, and as she burst through, Yuan Fei let out something between a yelp and a gasp when she saw me, almost dropping her cell phone and glass tumbler in the process.

'What are you doing, sneaking about in the dark? You scared the life out of me!'

I was a little startled myself, but maintained my composure.

'It was really quiet, so I decided to come check on you. I . . . well . . . wait, what's wrong?' I asked.

She averted her gaze as she came closer, although, when she reached for the countertop kettle, her despaired countenance was plain to see as she poured water over the Longjing leaves, moistening them for the umpteenth time, offering no explanation before returning to the living room.

I picked up the other glass of Longjingcha and followed behind her. It was lukewarm at best when I took a sip. Just how long had it been sitting there?

'Don't drink that,' she said, gazing across the lake as far as her eyes would allow. 'Someone's already drunk from it.'

'Oh? Do we have a visitor?' I asked, more curious than bothered that I was drinking from another's glass. She sighed, almost inaudibly.

'The sponsor dropped in . . . without a call or message or any fundamental sense of courtesy.'

'The representative you met with before?'

'Well, I suppose I've finally met the boss for the first time today: an old lady shrouded in mystery who can't seem to decide if she wants to dress more Margiela or Owens. Apparently, she just happened to be in the area and wanted to see how far I was getting along with my prints, although it sure felt like a landlord spot-checking on a tenant . . .' she trailed off.

I put down my glass and went to her.

'. . . let's just say she wasn't all that impressed and left in a hurry. Then, only moments later, she calls up for fear her intentions are misconstrued, and begins to explain her theories on photography, even saying she'll have her assistant bring me some *essential* reading materials.'

'She sounds like something else.'

Yuan Fei turned to face me and still in the darkness, her half-smile was incredibly fragile. In her eyes, though pained, I saw hope abundant, and could divine that there was nothing but pure grit in this woman. In the moment the sun set over the distant hills, I don't think I had ever felt closer to anyone before, and her every step away from me made my heart sink a little. But then, when I felt her reach back to guide my hand into hers, it felt as if any eventual distance between us would be negligible and every weight in this life felt a tad more bearable.

She led me by the hand all the way into her studio where, with the tap of a switch, she illuminated the two rows of fluorescent tube lights suspended from the ceiling. She soon let go and began putting away the heap of black-and-white A0 prints, which she had been showing her sponsor, back into the flat-file cabinet. I shielded my squinting eyes and turned to the other corner of the room where, propped on an easel, was a large canvas in what appeared to be a monochrome gradient, in which, from left to right, the spectrum of black and white tonalities ran from darkest to lightest. In the picture labelled *UHS 1* stood a subject standing on a desolate street— or standing desolately on a street depending on the way you looked at it—with the only source of light, save the burning cigarette tip, being the light trails from the bus that passed on from behind him. The subject's demeanour was predominantly male, a picture exuding an uncanny force with a face stuck in a blur of motion, an obscurity varying in shades of darkness. Such was the brutality of my countenance.

'This wouldn't happen to be me, would it?'

'Well,' came her curt reply, not taking her eyes off putting things away, 'if you must know, he's my poster boy.'

Poster boy? Now she was just winding me up.

Is this how she sees me? I wondered, seeing how obliterated my face had become, two halves of varying tonal depth, both cast in shadow. Was this how I appeared in the eyes of another?

Our kiss on the first night we met happened to be an idealization of sorts, a mutual realization of desire between two lonely individuals. But now, as Yuan Fei edged closer, bringing her arms around me from behind in warm embrace, I realized that the fulfilment of our desires depended on the pre-existence of a lack, without which one could potentially harbour an even greater frustration and unhappiness. Was I unhappy in my life? I didn't think so, not with her gently caressing my face with both hands and sliding her tongue in and out of my mouth, so that I entirely felt the softness of her lips against mine.

'This is the way I see you, the way I've always seen you,' she told me in bated, breathless whispers, as she then slithered one hand down my pants to grip my already throbbing cock.

With every stroke my desire grew, and with every kiss I wanted to taste more of her.

She undid my pants and pulled them off. Our gazes met, and she knelt down.

Only, when she placed me inside her mouth, I went soft. Like a pathetic skydancer, who couldn't withstand even a gust of wind.

Wasn't this what I had always wanted for so long?

Why couldn't I stay erect for her?

I brought her up and lifted her on to the tall standing desk, still cluttered with contact sheets, film rolls and bottles that I reached across and swept on to the floor in one swift motion. Yuan Fei didn't seem to care.

'Wait . . . turn on the safelight instead,' she said.

Eager not to delay things, I did as I was told, flicking the switches so the room turned a dark crimson. Then, appearing to read my mind, she pulled down her skirt, allowing me a glance at her wetness showing through her underwear—a spot I rubbed and fixated on, as if marking the spot to where I then took my tongue without reserve. She squirmed a little as I went down but, with my face pressing in only tentatively on the outside, I couldn't tell whether she found it pleasurable and so, to be sure, I deftly lifted her panties to one side and plunged in, making sure with every kiss and twirl of the tongue to savour the salt of her sex.

'Use your fingers . . .' she instructed, whilst running her hands through my hair to coax me further inside. I did as I was told and parted her hot lips with my fingers, steadying myself as I went in for another rendezvous with her swelling clit.

I had never wanted to please her more.

She freed herself from my arms and rose from the deformed bean bag, where we no longer lay abreast. I remember watching her go as the lights went out, shallow in my slumber, awaiting her return.

Chapter 19

I opened my eyes to the glare of morning sunlight pouring in through the windows, filling the bare room and revealing every blemish on the pallid walls of the studio.

Yuan Fei was gone. Seeing as a bean bag wasn't the most comfortable resting place for two people, I couldn't fault her, although I wasn't sure if she had left the previous night or early this morning.

I got up and rubbed chunks of crust from my eyes. Had I been out that long? Because it didn't feel that way. While pondering that thought, it occurred to me that we hadn't had dinner last night, the late afternoon coffee and jianbing being the only sustenance we'd had. Perhaps she had gotten hungry and left to order Waimai or to cook up that midnight aglio olio using Lao Gan Ma instead of the red-chilli flakes she enjoyed so much.

Strangely enough, I didn't feel like I had missed a meal—a literal and not a euphemistic one, of course. I thought I had better help tidy up the mess I had swept on to the floor before going about my day. I picked up scattered film canisters and then arranged the numerous bottles of chemicals neatly on the tray, relieved not to have spilt and wasted any when I had sent them flying off the table. I then reached for the loose contact-proofs and clasped them between the plastic folder with the masking-tape label marked *Tri-X*. Why not sneak a look inside?

I picked up the magnifier and took it to the contact sheet, mimicking what I had seen Yuan Fei do time and time again, and took my time with each sheet which contained 6 x 6 rows of black-and-white exposures.

Her scope of photography was very eclectic, and at times completely perplexing. There were several contact sheets full of photographs. I couldn't really fathom what she had sought to document in each frame. She would shoot objects such as a full bowl of noodles with a high-speed rail ticket from Beijing to Shanghai swimming right in the middle of it; or a complete series of shot-from-above pictures of an unopened six-pack of beer alongside four bottles of wine split in half through the middle, the cuts so clean they looked to have been done using a laser, corks still intact with black wine spilling all over. But then there were also rolls and rolls of high-contrast, realistic, street photographs, from a taxi driver entering a Mahjong parlour with his car parked handsomely out front, or a call girl standing on the street whilst shielding her face from the camera. My favourite was a series of some rather candid, high-contrast portraits of a powdered-up young lady in a designer robe as she exited a dingy flat, with one hand lighting a cigarette and the other wheeling her baby out on a stroller—perfect as a Smiths album cover, if you asked me. Yuan Fei had actually taken at least a dozen shots of the young woman, each and every one of them illustrating a different expression of motherhood. How she had managed to get so close without being spat on, I'll never know.

Here was the work of a bold and ruthless photographer, afraid neither of confrontation with her subjects nor the liberal usage of film on them. With her consistently averaging three to five shots per subject, I imagined that some of them must have found it upsetting to be photographed in this offhand manner. Was the invasion of personal space necessary to her artistic composition? Had the sponsor lady been upset by this controversial methodology?

Perhaps it wasn't my place to ask these questions which, at the end of the day, were merely academic for me. So, I filed the contact sheets away and that was when I saw a drawer sticking out loosely from a lateral-file cabinet. I pulled the drawer open fully and was surprised to see a colour photograph among all the other monochrome, A0-sized prints. The large print was a portrait shot of a veiled bride, who wore sunglasses beneath the long, fine tulle with her ash-grey hair braided to one side, except that the bottom half of the image appeared to have been burnt off, therefore obscuring her face. I was no expert but, having looked at contact sheets for the past half hour, I presumed this effect of having the edge of an image obliterated was due to the shot being the first of that film roll. It was a beautiful image, nonetheless. So beautiful that the more I looked at it, the more uneasy my thoughts turned within me.

I flipped the print up to view the second picture, and then the third. Sure enough, they were all of the same ash-grey-haired bride, although this time I could see her full face unveiled, clear as day in the brilliant sunlight.

Luna.

My heart stopped.

There was no doubt. Hers was a face I knew all too well.

Why was she haunting me all the way to Gao Yuan Fei's house?

I scrutinized the pictures for any hints about when Yuan Fei had actually shot these. Like a sleuth on to a new lead I tried to deduce from the bokeh'd-out background the city in which they had met, and whether it looked to be a pure chance encounter or a paid photoshoot. All the possible cities and likelihoods went racing through my head, and for a moment I not only conceded the possibility of their having not only a working relationship but also a romantic liaison. But these were merely sheer odds that I was running through my mind and that did naught in unravelling any truth because in that moment there was not one scenario that seemed impossible to me.

Were there more pictures of her?

Without an iota of shame, I was prepared to rummage through the rest of the filing-cabinet drawers for any semblance of an answer. File #31. That's where I saw everything—the pictures of Luna and the girl named Rei during their bridal shoot at Xujiahui Park, pictures of them kissing and seeing all in the other's eyes—pictures of them in love.

Then the sound of approaching footsteps down the corridor froze me, hastening the closing of file #31.

'Sleep well?' Yuan Fei asked, her head craned like a giraffe across the threshold. She came in holding two steaming cups of coffee and handed one to me. I sipped and managed something passable for a smile, even if the drink tasted just as insipid as it felt in my hands.

'What are you doing? Did you only just get up?'

My lips seemed to dry up with the coffee; I tried my best to speak.

'I've been up for a while; just thought I'd clean up a little first. The table was a proper mess.'

'Don't worry, I need to tidy things up and give the room a thorough sweeping later on anyway. You know, just as the *laowai* would do, *cleaning in the spring*.'

I said I would help her and then for a while, we just stood there in silence, sipping coffee.

'Actually, there's something I need to talk to you about,' she said.

'Okay.'

'I've been told to vacate the house as soon as I can.'

'What do you mean?'

'The sponsor pulled out. I just got off the phone with them on WeChat.'

I didn't know what to say.

'They can't simply do that, right? I'm sure it's against the law.'

'Illegal in China?' she laughed. 'It's her place and her money anyway. It's always the money which makes things ephemeral, like those flies that live for a day.'

Yuan Fei was calm as she spoke, but her eyes gave her away. She looked shattered and I should've gone ahead and held her in my arms, but all I could think of was the picture I had seen, of a woman I had never met and her lover, Rei, if that was indeed her real name, with whom I had gone on a Tinder date.

I set the cup of coffee down on the table we were no longer welcome to use, walked over to the cabinet and slid the drawer open.

I had this gut feeling.

'Is this lady your sponsor? Is she the one kicking us out?'

She looked bewildered, just as I was when I found the prints. Perhaps it was too early for questions. *What was I on about?*

'What do you mean? You do know that the sponsor—well it's not like she's sponsoring me any more—you know she's a well-ripened, middle-aged woman?'

I didn't respond and got closer to scrutinize the photograph. This was Luna, I had no doubts. But who was she? Luna and the Crescent Moon Dealership who were sponsoring Yuan Fei. I was sure they were all interconnected.

'I shot this a long time ago when I had chanced upon a couple of lesbian university students at Xujiahui Park. It was late summer, I remember, because I felt the bright sunlight would be great for shooting colour film.'

Luna and Rei were lovers, it was plain enough to see.

'Why are you digging about my work and asking all these questions? I just told you we have to leave here. Why is this picture so important?'

I couldn't give her an explanation. How was I even supposed to begin?

Yuan Fei shook her head, and then she left, frustrated.

I wanted to leave too, but where would I go? Back to Shanghai? Pay another security deposit on an apartment and go back to work? My visa had been renewed and I could stay on for a few more months if I wanted to, but what good would that do when I was to go back to becoming a shadow fading in with all the others? I hadn't spoken to my mother in a long time. What would she think of me—a boy who never brought her shame for he dared not even tread the whiter waters? I wanted to do more in this life for myself, to give more to the people around me. I wanted to find my dream through passion and not stumble in my footsteps by chasing the reverse. I wanted to reach out and touch real love, even if seizing it meant I would only hold it for a moment in my hands before it vanished.

I hadn't been doing any of that in China. Perhaps it really was time for me to go home.

I went back to my desk and picked up the journal KenSon had given me, flipping through the forty-odd pages I had written for Yuan Fei's artist biography over the last few months. I would've liked to polish and refine the text further before surrendering it to her—that is, if she still had any use for it at this point—but I was no longer in that literary space that allowed me to write about her; as if I had woken one morning on the other side of it, just as I had grown comfortable inhabiting it. I opened the word file and hit print, and just watched the white sheets sprout from machine into tray, an experience I always found hypnotic. All I heard was the sound of hot ink to paper, followed by her footsteps going down the hallway and out the front door.

I placed the journal on top of the heap of paper and left.

But I didn't get very far with my dramatic exit. The doors of the garage outside the studio were open, and I watched Yuan Fei pull off a grey cover-sheet from a metallic-turquoise coloured hatchback.

A Golf R. Nice. I wasn't a car expert, but this Volkswagen looked stock for the most part, except for the valved exhaust pipes and bronze-flow formed wheels. If the ride height had been lowered, it looked to have been minimal and no more than twenty millimetres.

'Get in. We can still make open track day if we hurry,' she said.

'Where are we going?'

'The racetrack. I literally just told you. Fast car, go vroom-vroom, you understand?'

'Ah? What about having to move out of the house right away?'

'Fuck it.'

Now wasn't the time to reason or argue with her.

'When do we have to be there? Shanghai Circuit is so far away.'

'You foreigners think a circuit must mean Shanghai, but there are new circuits popping up all over the country every year. We're going to Zhejiang International Circuit, sixteen turns over 3.2 kilometres, with an elevation of about twenty-two metres from the lowest to highest point, a picturesque track beside the Dongdanshan Park. You in?'

You foreigners, huh? I couldn't argue with that, but it still hurt, coming from her.

Before we left, she sent me inside to change into long-sleeved clothing.

'Be sure it's made of cotton, and don't wear shorts,' she said.

'And what about you?' I asked, doing a head-to-toe of her in sweatpants and tank top.

'I have a race suit in my track locker. Hurry up!' she said.

I washed up quickly, got dressed in jeans and a knock-off, long-sleeved Didier Drogba jersey from his time playing at Shanghai Shenhua, the only clean shirt I had lying around, put on a hoodie and got back into the car.

'Interesting choice of shirt; make sure you keep the hoodie zipped up at the track,' Yuan Fei said, and then wasted no time pulling out of the garage and exiting the stone gates of the compound. For a long time, we did not speak. With her slender hands firmly gripping the steering wheel and her foot steadily nursing the accelerator, she manoeuvred the car through the neighbourhood and brought us gliding past the food stalls and morning markets offering the day's fare. I peered out wistfully at all of the food but dared not ask her to stop. I hadn't slept much and the sounds of the bustling market and blaring morning traffic only aggravated my state of lightheadedness.

Yuan Fei, on the other hand, I could see was recharged and raring to go. Simply by being behind the wheel she felt more at ease and in control. Now completely relaxed, she was very different from the flustered woman in her studio this morning. In fact, I had never seen her this at peace and unthinking. Why hadn't we taken any drives before today? It felt great riding in the passenger seat, thanks to her every shift of the six-speed, manual gearbox being buttery smooth and seamless. She braked early before turning and knew where to avoid the plague of potholes. It was only after she pulled on to the highway that she really floored it and the sound of the exhaust roared in response to every perfect upshift.

'That's loud!' I yelled, struggling to hear my own voice over the drone of vibrations. She smiled, she could see I was new to this, a total virgin. She slowed down as she came up to the traffic ahead.

'That's a Milltek, non-resonated exhaust—meaning the sound from the engine passes straight through the pipes and out the back. There's no additional box-chamber that a resonated exhaust would have, so essentially, there's no silencer.'

'And the tyres?' I asked, trying to sound like I knew stuff.

'Hmm . . . Michelin Pilot Sport 4s, 235/35, nineteen inches in diameter. I like them. When the 5s come out, I might upgrade.'

'Do you do the mods yourself?'

She looked at me. The game was up, it was obvious I didn't know anything.

'With a little help from the mechanics down at the workshop, yeah.'

The traffic slowed to a crawl.

'Can I ask you about the photograph, the one with the beer and wine bottles?'

'What about it?'

'It seemed like a pretty deliberate set-up; I was just wondering if you were behind it?'

She sighed.

'Yes,' she said. 'It didn't quite turn out the way I liked it, for the very same reason you stated, its "appearing too deliberate". But at the same time, the deliberation is the whole point, because the way governments exert control over people, that's entirely deliberate too, isn't it? And how a people reacts in fear to these structures of power, that's deliberate too—although its being a deliberation is done out of necessity.'

'You're referring to 1989, to Tiananmen, right?'

'Obviously . . . but it's not only that. It's the whole idea of the end of the revolution and the end of history that is depressing; the death of punk rock, of film photography, of the publishing industry that we've already grown accustomed to and now have begun to romanticize. Following closely behind is the advent of the Internet and the necessary economics of mass production, causing climate change and the merging of neoliberalist political views held by millennials with what boomers like to call progressive conservatism. The lines that used to separate liberal and conservative are getting increasingly blurry.'

'And that would be quite difficult to show in a photograph, I can imagine.'

'Well, if it's a literal picture, then yes. But perhaps being an artist in China, not going the literal way would be the best.'

'What do you mean?'

She thought about it for a while. I took a risk and rummaged through her centre compartment, expecting to find a candy bar or two, but had to settle for some vacuum-sealed, smoked, duck tongues and claws. I ate them without asking.

'Take the Tiananmen Square Incident for example. The foreign press might be inclined to say that the State is suppressing any public discussion of the event, that the authorities are maintaining constant surveillance on everything from our WeChat chat logs to casual conversations we may have in public, also making sure historical accounts in published books old and new are in line with the State's strict standard of censorship. And while that may apply for the majority of regions in China, it would completely oversimplify the memory of these events for the residents of Beijing because, for them, the incident was a tragedy that happened to real people around them, somebody's grandfather might have killed another's grandmother. In these cases, what good would a literal and truthful account of the event yield? For a lot of people, the banality of everyday life surpasses the supposed truth presented in a political life.'

'Because being alive is all that matters?'

'We're talking about art, right? I would think that being alive is pretty essential to creating art, so yes.'

'I liked your picture even if the political connection to it was removed and if we took the image as a standalone in itself, so to speak.'

'But, you see, that's how I think all art is supposed to be taken. Art is political, but only insofar as the political awareness of an individual allows it. After an artist puts something out in the world, it's no longer theirs to mould and control. The artwork comes to take on a plastic nature, so to speak, as it has taken its form from the artist, and gives another form back to the individual viewer of the artwork.'

'So, you're saying: whether a piece of artwork is to be taken as radical or reactionary ultimately depends on how politically aware a person is?'

'Kind of.'

We approached a bunch of supercars on the highway. We must've been near the track.

'I'm thinking the relation of politics to art is kind of analogous to one's point of view on religion,' I said.

Yuan Fei laughed. How so? she asked me to elaborate.

'Well, you see, you kind of have to be religious in order to be an atheist, because atheism is based on disproving and rejecting the tenets of a religion. So, if we follow the same vein of thinking, you kind of have to have some measure of political awareness in order to deem an artwork as political, and vice versa with a piece that's non-political.'

'Hmm, I can see what you're saying . . . but what about people who are agnostic?'

'Well . . . people who are politically agnostic, believe that an outside life, completely independent of the political system is possible. They might believe that there's too much of history that cannot be known for certain, because according to them, history is always written by the victors who hold power. As for the future, they believe that human beings can never truly prepare for political contingencies as there is simply too much uncertainty lying within the future.'

'They might feel the upshots of government policies to be irrelevant, because they won't live to see its effects on a country's welfare.'

'Yes, exactly. The politically agnostic do not feel they have enough facts before them to judge and know for sure whether a human being should favour the Left or the Right; whether existence as a liberal is more worth it or, as a conservative.'

Yuan Fei laughed.

'Sounds like nihilism. It doesn't really work.'

'What about love, though?' I ventured. 'Can one be agnostic with regard to this fantastically real emotion, so fleeting in its every passing moment that we may consider it fickle? Is there a point where love existing in the eternal simply dissipates into the quotidian that one completely misses it?'

'No, there's no point being agnostic about love,' Yuan Fei said, turning the steering wheel with one hand and exiting the highway. 'Once you have it, you'll know it's real.'

Chapter 20

they are greeted with clear skies and beaming sunlight at the circuit such perfect track day conditions in late winter the chief instructor tells them at the briefing he says the first three turns are tight where cars can hardly make it through side by side so be aware of your surroundings do not get too excited before approaching the uphill section leading into turn four where on your left you'll be level with the grandstands now empty but feel free to imagine how magnificently packed it'll be on a race day as cars come over the crest before speeding down the slope towards turn five brake hard hugging the left kerb and you'll come to the lowest point of the circuit now which is also where the circuit can be split into east and west and for now we'll be heading west for turn eight with its constant radius scenic against the large wall of rocks our on-track photographers will use it as a backdrop to take some great pictures of you in your car if you desire but let's keep pushing on for now as we should always do in life and we'll come to perhaps the most challenging part of the circuit where the very tight turn nine goes into a downhill in a series of tight and tricky apexed turns ten eleven and twelve forming an S still going downhill you must brake hard before the hairpin of turn thirteen and get a good exit where you can pretty much go flat out on the back straight if you have enough downforce before coming around turn sixteen to take the chequered flag all right now so please only overtake on the left side of the circuit and if you're being overtaken signal to indicate the side you're moving to so that faster cars may pass and so Yuan Fei after she listens to the briefing she enters the locker room and she changes into red race suit red boots and red helmet as red is the colour of all and everything she likes about speed like the rev counter and the red-white kerbs and the red Brembo brakes of her Golf R which she now steps into is turquoise because the car is the only thing she doesn't want to be red lest it appear too garish for her to drive on the daily then she meets him at the pit lane and invites him to hop into the passenger seat beside her for the first few sighting laps of the circuit just to get a feel for what it is like on track before she does her hot laps which he obliges but not without some trepidation because he knows speed can kill even if drivers are wearing helmets and thermal gear and cars may come equipped with all sorts of air bags and reinforced frames for enhanced crash-protection but accidents still happen from time to time because of driver error or someone else on the track being a fucking idiot and not adhering to the rules or thinking they are Fernando Alonso going around the outside when there is scarcely any space to overtake another car but then perhaps less experienced drivers are unwary of accidental oil spillage or water seepage being released from beneath the track following heavy rainstorms due to poorly maintained drainage systems that simply do not work except as death-traps but Sofia she tells him not to worry not to fret not to feel fear because as Wittgenstein says death is not an event in life because we do not live to experience death and if one takes eternity not to mean infinite temporal duration and time but timelessness itself then eternal life shall belong to those who live in the present and our life has no end in the way in which our visual field has no limits but that doesn't make me feel any better he thinks because he isn't so much worried about death but the possibility of crashing and becoming a paraplegic or losing a limb or even going into a coma into a locked-in state where one is aware of one's surroundings but unable to move or speak out of the paralysis of voluntary muscles except for the blinking and eye movements is very real yet he does not make known his reservations about this casual something of a simple sighting lap around the circuit that she is so accustomed to doing because the changing gears and application of the brakes and throttle to her is something just as instinctual as adjusting the shutter speed or opening or closing the aperture on her mechanical camera and the art of judging braking points to her is just like estimating the range of pre-focus and shooting-from-the-hip techniques she uses on her rangefinder camera and on the first lap all is fine and dandy he is enjoying himself feeling the first instances of speed and G-force while Sofia cruises through the corners and over the kerbs and up the tight winding S chicanes but really she isn't pushing hard at all still trying to get a feel of how grippy the track is while there aren't many other cars on the circuit except for some Subarus and some Mercedes Benzes so while he is naturally feeling nervous from never going fast before he tells her to just go for it as they say when in doubt flat out isn't that what they say? sure she says not telling him that what he's saying is actually a Colin McRae reference from rallying that nearly killed the Scotsman many times anyway because she's in the zone now she starts speeding past the pit lane down into turn one hard braking as much as her car allows it little bit of understeer never hurt anyone then the S turns that she has never quite got the hang of so slowly does it as she pushes and observes how to use as much of the track and the kerbs as possible but in reality she isn't straying too far from the centre of the track before coming to the uphill section where she's her fastest somehow sending her car over the positive-sloped cambers feeling the centrifugal forces work the MacPherson strut suspension thrusting the tyres inwards and also being thrust around is his stomach now empty save for the few slices of duck tongues and claws he ate hastily in the car for breakfast now making him sick so sick he wants Pu'er tea to wash it down anything to keep it down a Maotai *baijiu* would make a good and hard last drink he thinks and calms down for a moment before she brings the car downhill and the car starts to slide in and out of the corners so close from hitting the barriers a sensation he has never felt before and the sight of her behind the wheel with eyes so focused is something he has never seen before either even when she is engrossed in her photography work her expression is contained in her brows twisted in melancholy but now her gaze is piercing and fixed purely on the track and nothing else she becomes one with the machine and one with the road leaving no room for error no time for hesitation and no deliberation so everything goes great for them for a couple of laps and he's getting used to it but then out of nowhere a Bug Eye Subaru WRX STI on a hot lap makes a sudden lunge down the inside of turn thirteen forcing her to swerve to the right abruptly on to the dirt side of the track and before she knows it they're sliding towards the barriers and so she hits the brakes and downshifts while struggling to correct the car but the rear pops out and she oversteers and spins to a halt what an asshole she thinks still maintaining her composure but he wasn't ready for that incident at all and his face is white with panic and he begins to feel sick and uneasy in his stomach and chest so she looks at him and thinks oh no is he going to throw up is he going to start spewing vomit in my car? can't stop on track would red flag the session would get penalized and lose face he must know I like him and everything even with all his insecurities and peculiarities but if he throws up in my car that changes a great deal and I wouldn't like to take the risk and so Sofia quickly gets going again but she's still on the back straight three turns away from the pit lane so she floors the throttle only lifting slightly on the last two kinks on the circuit before she's finally able to decelerate into turn sixteen and bring her hot hatch into the pits but before she can come to a complete stop she hears him vomiting into his visor and she really dares not look but the smell starts to permeate her car and she reaches over to wind down the windows but it's of no use the stench of his puke is overwhelming and then she begins to get gag reflexes too but what can she do at this point but force herself to maintain her composure exit the car and move to help him but how can she help a man who is past the point of continence as she pulls him out wearing a freshly soiled Didier Drogba jersey in Hangzhou on top of that thinking this is not how a man in love should behave at all but she looks after him even when in his state of post-nausea he gains a sense of ultra-consciousness and begins to have visions of Luna Luna as the idealized one as he first dreamed of her being with him together who would move back to Malaysia with him together buy a piece of land of one or two acres somewhere in the kampung still within an hour's driving distance to the city to live a happy yet simple life living off the land planting D24 durians or the Musang King variety perhaps even mangosteens and whatever else the mainland Chinese fancied where they could build a humble abode like in those tiny house videos she liked to share with him living-off-the-grid that is what they called it also doubling as a perfect base from where they could travel Asia to see Saigon and the Independence Palace to Angkor Wat and Borobudur where she wanted to see how the temples had been restored then to Pai for the hot springs and the waterfall as she adored being near water as she would say then they would go to Taman Negara where he wanted to show her the oldest rainforest in the world a fact most Malaysians are not aware of and she said she would return the favour bringing him to Sêrtar County in Sichuan Province told him not to worry because she could get him in even if he was on a Malaysian passport and he was happy and he pictured going to all these places and experiencing them with her by his side her with her lurid tattoos in cubist forms which he couldn't fathom but liked all the more her chameleon hair her mercurial wardrobe and everything she was he wanted and desired she who promised him everything and at the same time nothing at all because it was all on him to first make his journey to China so they could meet up and he would see her the real one he thought he was in love with and who he thought was in love with him too Luna in all her mystery and digital sensuality in her art and her poetry and her humour the way she made him feel about himself the way she was simply just everything that he was not for she was Luna the other as he had imagined her but never saw whose real name he doesn't even know but yes it is her her her who appears to walk towards him now with her green hair leading him away from their meeting point at the corner of Hengshan Lu and Wanping Lu and she gives him her hands and they walk and walk while she begins a solemn recital of part of the Li Sao by the poet Qu Yuan she says the day passes into night unstagnant spring autumn are in order trees flowers fall scattered fearing the twilight of beauty repress not the sordid in youth for what reason not to change this law? riding steed in canter and gallop come I will show you the way and he replies am aware loyalty brings about disaster want to endure it but never within control calling the nine heavens to witness fidelity in a spirit unchanging for the lord was agreed to join in blood relations at dusk though for unknown reasons the path changed in place of a first promise now other plans bring a regretful release left is not sadness in parting what is painful is the back and forth left are the orchids in spring hundreds of acres of Qiuhui peony plantago asiatica horseshoe incense and angelica and she grips his hand tighter and says looking back into past and now to future fundamental truths of being are revealed there are no unrighteous acts to commit there are no unkind matters to undertake even in the face of death have no regrets of the ideal as sockets pared down without first aligning the chisel make the wise men of the past suffer and he replies sobbing constantly a troubled mind in sadness laments the fact a good time was never had now rubs eye with soft holy basil while hot tears wet garments slowly with collars spread and kneeling down the right path is obtained with a bright heart and riding the horned Qiulong phoenix carriage in the winds taking me to the skies but eventually he can no longer channel the spirit of Qu Yuan and must return to earth where he finds himself embracing her in the middle of the sycamore-laden streets of Xuhui with their long branches forming hollow shadows and the wintry wind billowing the leaves in every direction he expects to feel the promise of her warmth her touch her forbidden intimacy but in place of all that he had hoped and longed for there is only an icy chill and so he lifts his head to look at her vanishing face and her fading body and once more now now now he is again a nothing he realizes in the immediacy of the moment that he is not meant to live the existence of a poet as he is not meant to inhabit the life of a loneliness of which he has experienced all and everything to do with it because as he looks up to the skies he sees Mercury masquerading as a star and it isn't often one sees stars in Shanghai he thinks so yes it must be and thus it cannot be otherwise that he is Mercury and will wear the mask of a planet amongst stars forever and therefore becoming greater than the great universal loneliness that has long been chasing him like a shadow.

come now come he hears a voice call out to him from beyond the street corner, a woman as far as he can tell by the soft and slightly accented tone of voice, come the voice beckons and then he hears it again shortly after

he pats down his pockets rummaging through them for anything, but they are empty and so with his head down he turns the corner to come face to face with the sales assistant from Betelnut Valley, the sales assistant of Li ethnicity dressed in her traditional collarless attire dyed red and gold with silver bracelets on each of her wrists and a silver necklace with tassels around her neck, she asks him if he is hungry and he nods, she asks if he fancies some hot pot and he nods once more, and without saying anything she turns and leads him to a hot-pot restaurant that seems to have appeared right behind her as if her invitation had just manifested it, she smiles and they enter the hot-pot restaurant with the interior of a cowboy saloon complete with double-swinging café doors and a bar stocked full of whiskey and bourbon with their labels torn off, and hanging from the ceiling rack is an array of stained glasses chipped and scratched here and there, the rest of the bar is a motley decoration of red lanterns and a papier-mâché wall plastered full of antithetical Chinese couplets, the sales assistant shows him to his round table and leaves for the kitchen area, with nobody inside the restaurant he is left to read the red rice-paper couplets that make little sense to him for they are written in a classical Chinese that is way beyond him, soon he realizes they aren't actually antithetical couplets and if he is to guess it is a tale of death and tragedy and just as well he has given up on deciphering it because the kitchen doors swing open and Li the sales assistant comes back wheeling a trolley with an assortment of red meat and fish sliced thin and then plated in the shape of flower petals also skewered kidneys tongues livers and whatever else constitutes as offal and then the pièce de résistance is a large yinyang pot with a pig and dragon head for handles, filled on one side with a clear pig's stomach soup and the other with a mala soup packed with dried chilli peppers Sichuan peppercorn scallions and loads of Chinese spices et voilà will you be needing anything else? she asks after lighting the stove and he says just jasmine rice and she says for sure right away and at the slightest hint of bubbling within the mala soup he starts the transferral of food by way of chopsticks into the red chilli soup quickly gurgling with peppers wondering why mala chilli soup always boils faster than clear broths probably because of the salt and fat content in the latter raising its boiling point but even with that explanation he would still like to put it down as one of the world's greatest mysteries for what else can he ponder while waiting on its boiling what else would he do with the amount of time the boredom the mundane nature of everyday life confronting him in every moment, he takes another look at the writings on the wall and the sales assistant who has been standing by all the time out of sight appears and she tells him that those are lines from the Peking opera The Case of Chen Shimei telling the tale of a truly heartless man who was married to the fragrant lotus Qin Xianglian, and he says all right why is he cruel and despicable and heartless he asks her and she begins to narrate quite-matter-of-factly the story of Chen Shimei who was a poor scholar who left his wife and children in the countryside to take the imperial examinations in which he would place first and as a result become an official of the emperor, and so without any conscience or heart he betrayed his faithful wife by marrying another woman and this other woman was actually the emperor's sister so who could blame him? but yes that is how tragedies tend to unfold and then he even tried to get his bodyguard and aide Han Qi to murder the one whom he once called his fragrant lotus although now that was only a name to him, heartless he says yes he was truly heartless she says, he even cost Han Qi his life because he on the other hand was actually a man of conscience who was unable to carry out his imperial duty and so he ended up taking his own life by cutting his own neck in a temple she says but your hot pot is beginning to boil so I better leave you to it she says, no I want to hear all of it he says putting more food into the clear bubbling pig's broth and she says well Qin Xianglian brought Han Qi's sword before Bao Zheng in court as evidence of Chen Shimei's ordering his bodyguard to commit murder and upon examining the sword he went into a fit of rage that heartless man and he lunged towards his wife no longer his fragrant lotus so Bao Zheng saw this as proof that he was indeed guilty and sentenced his neck to be met with the bronze to be beheaded by way of the dragon-head guillotine she says but he is unwavering in his gaze focusing on every character of classical Mandarin, each of its brushstrokes so familiar yet entirely foreign when arranged in monosyllabic nature with its tendency to nominalize phrases making nouns out of verbs and adjectives not to mention its absence of numeral measures for objects and aversion of the regular first person pronouns so common in modern Chinese, and then there is the elliptical omission of the subject in speech and writing how did anybody ever manage to converse in this manner he wonders could that be why people see Chinese people as timid and reserved owing to over 3,000 years of not saying I he wonders, and then the flashbacks happen and he is back in his forlorn vernacular Chinese school classroom becoming indoctrinated with the language of the people known as *baihua* as a result of the May Fourth Movements and yet in the same class students are also required to learn and expected to master the *wenyanwen* of the old Chinese so that the literary culture is not forgotten and he thinks oh why god why does being Chinese have to be so difficult?

he tries to focus on the writing in itself but this language on the wall so old and out of reach cannot possibly belong to him, and so he doesn't really know what to make of the sales assistant's summary of The Case of Guillotining Chen Shimei and goes back to his food for a moment thinking it must have gone cold by now but no how can food in a bubbling hot pot actually go cold? he doesn't think and only eats as if he has undertaken a great important task so she leaves him to it although not forgetting to extend an invitation, she says if he wishes to know more about the opera there will be a show shortly afterwards should he like to stick around for quite the immersive performance of a lifetime she says but he just eats and eats and eats for fear the food will get cold as he has this hatred for the lukewarm, and in his gluttony he breaks all the rules and disregards all the etiquettes of hot-pot eating, mixing the ladles and utensils getting oily chilli in the clear broth and neglecting to cook the vegetables like radishes and potatoes long enough so they are practically al dente with too much bite to them which is most sacrilegious to the ritual of enjoying hot pot because one should really take their time with cooking the ingredients, and he knows the sales assistant whose silhouette he can make out from the corner of his eye must be shaking her head in disapproval that he is treating hot pot as a stew by cooking everything at once but as long as he can eat it all fast enough he'll be fine he thinks

now as the cowboy restaurant fills up rapidly she enters in black following the sea of people thronging in through the saloon doors just in time for the opera performance, she takes her usual seat at the bar across from his table and orders her drink of choice a bottle of ten-year-old yellow wine called Nü Er Jiu meaning the daughter's wine and pours it into a porcelain cup to admire the sparkle of the silky caramel-coloured liquid one sip before downing it straight, and there from the high stool she watches him try to fill up his stomach wolfing down bowl after bowl and he is so fixated on eating that he does not see her, now more waiters appear from the backroom to serve the guests their food and drinks and the place is properly full and buzzing with energy

but it quickly hushes over as soon as the woody sounds of the clapper drums and *paiban* flat board quicken to signal the beginning of the performance, echoing across the room to gradually build a palpable sense of suspense amongst the audience, and with the distinct sound of the metal gong or *xiaoluo* rising so magnificently in contrast to the descending pitch of the crashing *jingbo* cymbals, the shrill piercing fiddle of the *jinghu* enters to complete the ensemble, with a sense of wonder he lifts his head up from eating and allows himself to be taken away by the sweet rhythmic sounds of the *luogudianzi*, awestruck and mesmerized by the bright but warm tones of the silk-stringed jinghu, but where are these sounds originating? in a corner of the room he sees seated on a dimly lit stage the Peking opera ensemble dressed fairly unassumingly in suit and tie, and the lights slowly come on when a familiar-faced singer takes the stage, emerging to nasally project the opening lines of the drama, and to his surprise the one making the crowd roar in excitement is KenSon decked out in python robe and a spread-horned headwear, wearing an intricate mask bearing a crescent moon to cover his forehead, except he appears to be in a trance fully enthralled in gaze, as if he sees not the audience before him but Kaifeng Palace of the Northern Song Dynasty, and he is Bao Zheng himself confronting the wretched and heartless Chen Shimei, he sings

O prince consort listen carefully, remember the Dragon Boat Festival in celebrating the emperor, where me and you spoke in the courtroom, at the mention of your marriage you looked unsettled, I assumed you might have a wife where you came from, and now mother and son have come to seek you out, so why do you lie and not recognize them? I advise you to do the right thing and recognize Xianglian, for when misfortune comes too late it is to regret

and KenSon sustains the last note in regret for a few more measures causing the crowd to cheer with a round of applause, and the ensemble breaks into refrain with a luogudianzi rhythm that gradually slows to a stop, but then the silk-stringed fiddle of the jinghu begins to pick up the tempo once more, and he continues

Prince consort there is no need to flatter us with your words, the evidence is now in the courtroom, people have come and seen the account of Xianglian

the rhythm of the luogudianzi quickens almost to double time, and along with the fiddle of the jinghu, he sings

Prince consort come take a closer look, it says Qin Xianglian thirty-two years old, is suing the imperial family's prince consort, for deceiving his majesty and misleading the emperor, broke his marriage vows to marry into royalty, attempted to murder his wife and kill his heirs without conscience, forced Han Qi to his death in a temple, she stamped this accusation on to the grand halls, why do you lie through gritted teeth?

the place erupts at the end of the performance, the restaurant is full of electricity, with people banging their fists on the tables and raising their glasses in great reverence to KenSon and the ensemble, for putting on a moving performance they begin to toast him, but to a greater degree their offerings of blessings and accolades are intended for the figure of Bao Zheng himself, as a cultural symbol of the just the humane and the benevolent, and KenSon can do nothing but continue to bow with gratitude and grace as if he is the Justice Bao incarnate

as the ensemble takes leave the restaurant quietens once more, and he notices at some point during the performance the flame beneath his hot pot was turned off leaving the soup to congeal into oily clumps of chilli and the black tripe he does not fancy, he pokes at the food with his chopsticks but ingesting it would do his stomach a great disservice, the waiter sees he is done and clears his table in no time then asks if he would like anything for dessert, no thank you I'm stuffed as *full died* he says, how about a digestif? like some Maotai made from fantastic sorghum with intricate floral notes? we also have huangjiu that is like sherry, or sambuca or grappa with espresso, the waiter offers, no thanks but do you have teh tarik? he asks

I'll ask the boss and see what I can do, says the waiter before leaving, and he looks all around wondering whatever happened to the Li sales assistant who coaxed him into the restaurant earlier and over his shoulder he sees a waitress and he asks her if the Li sales assistant had gotten off her shift already, but she just smiles and looks a little confused and he realizes this is her now dressed in black-and-white just like any other regular waitress would and now without her silver necklace and bracelets she looks rather regular like any Chinese person in the restaurant, and he notices the waiter has gone over to the lady in black at the counter whom he recognizes as the sponsor except this time her ashen hair is highlighted blonde, and the waiter lowers his head now probably to ask about that cup of teh tarik, the sponsor nods and turns her head in his direction and through her big bee sunglasses their eyes meet and she raises her glass of Nü Er Jiu to him and he reaches for the only drink on his table a clear glass of water and raises it back in return, and then KenSon who is now dressed as a cowboy again with his chambray shirt and jeans with commando-soled brogues goes over to where the sponsor is sitting and leans over to kiss her, and he feels a great urge to go over and do something like grab KenSon by the shoulders and slap some sense into him perhaps warn him of the dangers of this woman who is caressing him so softly with her tongue down his throat and her hand sliding down his pants, but he feels there is no point as he has no words at this point only running on emotions, and finally after they stop kissing KenSon sees him and his eyes widen and the two of them move over to sit at his table and he doesn't know what to say so he like everyone else commends KenSon on the performance and KenSon just says thank you for being so kind it's so good to see you here of all places, then he asks KenSon how long he has been learning the art of Jingxi and KenSon shrugs and says he has perfect pitch and that helps quite a lot, then the waiter brings them three cups of teh tarik with a perfect ratio of bubbles to tea and he is so impressed he is unconcerned about starting up a conversation and so the three of them just sit there for the longest time drinking their sweet tea in silence and then KenSon goes ahead and puts his hand around the sponsor and says this here is my xianglian, my fragrant lotus, and she smiles and says she would much prefer if he called her his flower of the mountain and he then laughs when she calls him her dearest bao bao who is everything but justice itself, and she explains that this is her newest venture she only decided to try out after dating KenSon and it was he who gave her this whole idea of a wild west saloon bar cum hot-pot restaurant so everyone here could thank KenSon for it, and this makes KenSon laugh and he says it was

her her her who saved him when he was down in the doldrums
with nowhere else to go and well he didn't even believe in himself
back then but then he met her and this changed his entire life yes
she did he says

she laughs and laughs at this and she says overseas Chinese
are so interesting, so what might your name be? she asks him

I wasn't aware we were supposed to do names here, he replies

come on KenSon has told me all about the overseas Chinese
culture but it's the names I'm always coming back to, I find
them all so interesting what with all the different dialects and
everything she says

you can just call me Chen Shi Mei he says, and they all laugh
and KenSon begins to give him this look to cut it out because she
is asking him a serious question being the big boss and everything
so the least he could do is to show a little respect

come on be serious, she says

no that is me Chen Shi Mei the greatest douchebag of all
douchebags he says, I am the cunt among cunts who womanizes
and will kill whichever son he should happen to father

and if you have a daughter? she asks in anger

and if I should have a daughter I would not hesitate to make a
whore of her just like Pan Jinlian the golden lotus, he says

that is absurd! she's a promiscuous femme fatale! she exclaims

I have no problem with a Pan Jinlian or being a Chen
Shi Mei, for they are the characters that humanity champions in
the romanticizing of prostitutes and the martyring of tyrants,
in fact nobody can and should judge them! like them, I will
only answer to the Mandate of Heaven if it is revealed to me,
how long has it been since the Chinese have faced that divine
revelation? he asks

do not conflate fiction and reality, the Mandate of Heaven is
very real KenSon warns him, his voice becoming stern as though
he were once again channelling the spirit of Bao Zheng

what would your mother think if she heard you speaking like this? Xianglian the fragrant lotus asks

there's no shame in what I've said, he insists, I'm a feminist who supports a radical reading of the tale of Pan Jinlian, he replies

don't be conned by his words! a voice calls out, he's a feminist who suffers from acute heteronormativity, says his editor from *TRIESTE* sitting at another table

that is no fault of mine! it was the way I was brought up! he protests

I say he's guilty! guilty of not being able to get it up! yells Sofia from another table

he couldn't even tell that I was a lesbian! hello peek the rainbow emoji! said Rei from another table

off with his head! and his limp dick! yells the one he imagines to be Luna, who has her arms wrapped tightly around Rei's shoulders

Bao Zheng is standing tall once more in his python robe and spread-horned hat, his crescent moon mask shines even in the dim lighting, he raises his hands in a beckoning motion, and from the kitchen behind him come the court officials wheeling out a pig's head guillotine, which they plonk down in the middle of the room, and he is hauled from the table and forced to kneel before the judge

he hears the familiar rhythm of the luogudianzi, and every chime of the xiaoluo rises to fill the air with a sense of perversion

bring the one who wishes to be known as Chen Shi Mei forward to hear his sentencing! make no mistake that this man is no martyr, he who dares challenge the Mandate of Heaven and insult the Lady Xianglian! the one who is not only a closet misogynist but an out and out misanthrope who hates humanity! you are not only guilty of swiping right too many times on Tinder, but also of harassing and haranguing the poor lonely women who pitied you enough to listen in the first place! and for having a limp dick even after taking aphrodisiacs is inexcusable! for that I sentence this pig to death by the pig-head guillotine! one which we have specially forged for scum like you!

after Bao Zheng reads out his sentence they pull him forward, and they force his head to rest on the lurid pink body of the pig, under the overhanging blade of the guillotine soon to befall him

any last words?

society moulds boys into Chen Shi Mei only for women to hate him the most, yet when a girl becomes Pan Jinlian she is most desired by men, isn't that ironic? he says

and even facing death he utters nonsense!

off with his head!

you will be cancelled!

and the entire heft of the blade is brought down on him.

Chapter 21

Gao Yuan Fei is loading her Leica M3 with a roll of Kodak Gold 200 film. She stands by her bedroom window threading the end of the 35mm film through the take-up spool, feeding the cassette into the camera body while making sure it aligns with the sprockets. This is something she has done an infinite number of times, but somehow going through these motions feels different today. Perhaps it has been way too long since she shot on colour film after so many projects using exclusively monochrome, or perhaps she is just hopeful for the day's beginning. She closes the bottom cover and begins to advance the film using the lever action and feels relieved she doesn't have the urge to smoke a cigarette which she has finally managed to give up. Apart from cigarettes, she has also grown tired of shooting medium-format cameras of late, so worn out from lugging those cumbersome devices all the way around Shanghai and to Hangzhou and back.

I'm just like an over-wrung piece of cloth, she thinks.

But today, she feels good she's shooting her first love that is 35mm film, and she thinks that at some point she should go back to a cheap and bare-bones point-and-shoot with an automatic flash and just go crazy, perhaps that would even make a great exhibition in itself someday, she thinks.

She stuffs several rolls of Portra 400 and CineStill 800Tungsten into her bag, colour films of faster ISO speeds more sensitive to light, for later in the day when the light will fade.

She knows there's nothing like using a good, metered flash for shooting in lowlight, but doesn't bring one as she wants to pack light for the day. She feels a flash always draws too much attention to herself anyway.

Yuan Fei steps out of her apartment and feels the unveiling of infinite possibilities within the morning sunshine.

Should she first grab a croissant and a long black from Baker & Spice, or go try out that new doujiang youtiao franchise popping up all over Shanghai? And when was the last time she mindlessly browsed a bookstore and read whatever she wanted, without having to research how digital cameras achieve zone focus by detecting high-contrast zones, or how smartphones use a kind of passive autofocus based on pixel contrast? When was the last time she wasn't pressed to read up on some new and quirky method of film development that used either caffenol, beer, wine, washing soda or vitamin C as solvents in their recipes to achieve a more sepia or violet toning, with the expectation that she could replicate the same result in her studio? Today, she is free to read up on any topic she likes. She immediately thinks of Vivian Maier—how great would it be to spend the morning delving fully into her work and what little is known of her life, her photographer's consciousness of the everyday, her sense of appreciation for cities, her sensibility for capturing images of people existing on the outside of rich America, all of which culminated in her aesthetic of casual, street photography? Her breath was taken away the first time she encountered Maier's work and she still gets goosebumps scrolling through the archive on her eponymous website. She has long admired this woman who worked for more than forty years as a nanny, yet still managed to produce more than 1,20,000 negatives in her lifetime. Many of these negatives hadn't been developed when she died an old lady in relative obscurity, with the bulk of her work only discovered when she failed to pay for her storage space on the Chicago North Side; her negatives, prints and audio recordings then auctioned before being published to posthumous critical acclaim. Maier took great photos, minded her own business for eighty-three years and left the photography world in awe of her extraordinary talent. How was this possible? Photography was her means of documenting and recording life, and she did it solely for herself. She had never tried putting her work out there, because she may not even have thought of it as work, Yuan Fei surmises, often reminding herself of this fact before embarking on a new project. Maier continues to be an inspiration to her, and she reveres her as a genius unknown and undiscovered in her own time. Unlike Kafka, there was no instruction to destroy her work, and she seemingly just forgot about it as she grew older. What a great way to live and to go, almost as if she were invisible. Isn't that how all artists ought to live? *Am I too young or too old to become a nanny photographer now that I'm in my thirties? Surely, I have a Rolleiflex 3.5T lying around somewhere?* she thinks.

And if she wants, she could even pick up a collection of Meng Haoran Tang poetry and spend the morning wallowing in the beauty of his landscapes, immersing herself in his writings depicting idyllic villages or boats on rivers in the autumn twilight. No matter how many times she encounters the text, she will still be left in awe at the way he expresses sorrow within the colours of an autumn sunset without once using words of sorrow, and at the sense of intimacy he manages to create under the open sky in the wilderness, where the moon hangs and the universe is tranquil in that very moment. *How do poets capture the beautiful with such grace? Can I replicate that in a photograph?* she wonders. Sometimes she would even pick up an English translation and read it beside the original classical text, but the sense of contrast and antithesis between each line in the text, will always remain untranslatable to her.

The exiled Yuan Shiyi has to face the injustice of early plum blossoms in Dayuling; this is contrasted with the incomparable spring in Meng Haoran's Luoyang.

Where has all of that beauty gone?

No. Each translation constitutes a new piece of writing in itself, she concludes.

A message comes in on her phone, then another, and another. She pulls out her phone, annoyed at the all too familiar sounds of Tinder messages, so full of hope at first, but only ever giving disappointment, she wishes she could change the ringtone but cannot be bothered. Alan wants to meet her for coffee on a Monday afternoon and asks where she'd like to go—loser. Pierre leaves her a list of all his favourite novels and movies of all time and now asks for her list—trying too hard. Last night, Xiang asked her out for drinks at 1 a.m.—*diaosi* creep. She mutes her phone and puts it on vibrate, convinced that the normal man is elsewhere, anywhere but on these apps.

She goes on walking, and walking. Why not go check out the contemporary art galleries on Yuyuan Road? She remembers the pink and playful Fiu Gallery, the graphic design exhibitions by European artists showcasing new shapes and colours jumping out at you, and the experimental installations by quirky fashion brands hoping to reach the young and discerning consumer through different and more interactive ways. She remembers the vibrance and the colours there, the cafés and boutiques in newly gentrified lilongs first constructed as a hybrid of the English row-house and traditional Chinese courtyard, where domestic life and social life in the courtyard were once elegantly divided. Now the area throngs full of influencers, queuing for pictures they will heavily filter in order to feed their social-medial existence, with couples holding their hands in love as they march in the shadows of the *shikumen lilongs* where famous dead people once went about their daily lives. She remembers the infinite gift shops and knick-knack stores catering to the tourist-residents of Shanghai, where the young and the hip congregate outside under the lights and promise of late October, chatting under the turning trees and smoking cigarettes, with the smell of rain drying on the asphalt beside them.

Winter's end is soon approaching, and after that yet another Spring Festival will come. Does she have another October in Shanghai left in her? Suddenly she becomes painfully aware of the transience of Chinese life.

She stops in her tracks, realizing she's just wandering mindlessly without having taken even one photo. The urge to spontaneously walk the streets in search of subjects to shoot has all but left her and now, being overcome with an inexplicable listlessness, she doesn't feel like doing anything at all. The window of morning sunshine has passed and the cold hits her to the core. She looks around and grabs a coffee from the first café she sees, thinking no, she doesn't need a cigarette. Now, she'll weigh her options. She doesn't have her car, which was parked at her parents' in Hangzhou. She can either continue in futility or cut her day off short and resign herself to get some work done in her studio at the 1933 Shanghai Slaughterhouse, to which she had relocated after being evicted from the Xihu lakeside residence some months ago. While she doesn't mind the brutalist aesthetic of the pre-communist abattoir with its many flights of winding Escheresque staircases, it isn't a workspace she sees herself using long term as she is only occupying the studio as a subtenant who agreed to take over the lease at a discount from her friend who, upon finding work in Marrakesh as a photojournalist, had up and left for North Africa without thinking twice about it. The studio was spacious and well equipped enough but, in reality, Yuan Fei had only agreed to see out the period of tenancy as a favour to her friend, who also needed help in dealing with the tail ends of some commercial shoots for retail-store openings, galleries and fashion shows. Yuan Fei had already decided to take a break from creative work and so this whole arrangement fell into place quite naturally. She hadn't shot digital cameras for a while and it took some time getting used to how quickly she was able to examine a raw image on her LCD screen, having just framed it moments ago using the electronic viewfinder. After a brief period of adaptation, she came to appreciate the fast-paced workflow, and the work became fairly straightforward and easy for her. The money was good, and she soon found herself taking on more jobs than she had intended. While the work itself was not tiring, Yuan Fei found the social side of it particularly draining. Clients would expect her to arrive early to a shoot for pointless briefings so they could 'get to know her' first; and then, after they got to know her, she would still be invited to attend countless after-parties and cocktail receptions on the pretext that she should socialize and get to know more prospective clients. She tried her best to squeeze everyone into her schedule, accepting jobs that were in the same vicinity so she could seamlessly work one job following the other. There would be the occasional difficult client, either unreasonably demanding or just plain rude, but she was always well-compensated for her efforts to accommodate them, and so she couldn't really complain.

Nobody had forced her to take on extra work, but she grew so accustomed to it that she began to neglect the more creative film projects she had planned to pursue. Slowly but surely, she became sucked into the world of stable work and regular wages. Soon, she would completely forget about exhibiting in Berlin, and about applying to the artist residencies in Singapore or Seoul. Soon, she would become one of those people who just enjoys the accumulation of money, saving frugally but never spending a single cent.

Her friend had her trapped now, hadn't she? Yuan Fei was happy she had jumped at the opportunity to work in North Africa but, to a greater extent, she had grown deeply jealous of her. She remembers it was about a year ago when her friend read Sanmao's *Stories of the Sahara* for the first time, and she couldn't stop raving about it. She strongly recommended everyone in their circle of friends to read this memoir of a travel book, for the sense of mystique which the barren desert gave off and for all the promises of romanticism contained within a foreign land, all told from the point of view of a free-spirited Chinese woman. But the truth was, they had all read it a long time ago as teenagers and had long since moved past the book, and being boring and responsible adults, they didn't think so much of it. Even though her friend never admitted it, Yuan Fei knew Sanmao was the reason she had applied for jobs in North Africa. When seeing her off at the airport, Yuan Fei could see the purity of joy coursing through her body and the excitement she could barely contain in her eyes. *How simple it was for a dream to touch and change a person, making them so properly brave, headstrong and stubborn,* she thought. *After more than a decade of working in Shanghai, reading a book was all it took for her to up and leave.*

Yuan Fei was envious of her decisiveness to no end. She couldn't understand how these life-altering transitions could happen so smoothly for people like her friend, who seemingly didn't have to try hard at all because it was pre-destined that they should get what they want as long as they wanted it bad enough. As Yuan Fei grew older, she found it harder to make these spontaneous decisions. Since when had she changed and become so tentative with everything? It seemed as though she would struggle for approval even from herself.

What was it that Confucius had said in his analects—that at fifty she will come to know what the heavens have destined for her? But why should her life be centred around this obsession of finding destiny? And why does she have to wait until sixty for her ears to be perfectly in tune, when even now she hears with perfect clarity the ugliness of the world? Why does she have to wait until the ripe age of seventy before she can follow the desires of her heart, without exceeding its capacity in any measure?

Fuck it. This makes no sense at all, she says.

I've never needed destiny in my life, she concludes.

And what should they expect to pursue in life once their days of being young have gotten away from them? Will they hold on to their capacities to dream, to desire and to be open to new senses of wonder? Will they still feel the tides of movement of their generational existential angst and try to find resolution before their selfhoods become permanently forced out of them by a society so hurried and eager to affix and tighten the nooses around their necks? Or will they just accept the fact that civilizations will create societies, and in turn societies will continue to create subjects who are expected to surrender their individualities for the good of civilizations? Will they choose an adult life that affords them with financial stability allowing them to buy anything they want, the caveat being: the responsibility of having a job and the necessary incurring of debt? Will their authentic selves prevail in a world where everyday life as they know it must come to be replaced by an economical life, in which, subsequently and eventually, a familial life will be expected of them, entailing the unavowable pressure of procreating for the sake of familial succession? How were they supposed to rationalize the weight and the absurdity of this culture?

He cannot bring himself to contemplate such matters any longer. For him, his goal is more immediate, that is to rid himself of unhappiness, to be free of the shadow of endless dread that stalks him all day and throughout the wee hours. He begins to think it's silly of him to even think he could ever be without it, knowing that the erasure of unhappiness would not equate to his actually being happy. For him, unhappiness exists as a wound that is his and only his, and never was it meant to be something to be taken away by another. He would prefer not to burden anyone with it.

Throwing up in Yuan Fei's car at the circuit has changed him. The incident has shaken him up so badly that he simply cannot bring himself to face her, and so he swiftly packs up what little belongings he has, including his new sandals which he will now wear for the first time, and vanishes from Hangzhou. On the train, he remembers how he had awakened mired in a foetid haze, completely perplexed at how he managed to get back to the lakeside residence, not remembering at all how he passed out after emptying his stomach of the duck tongues and feet he had consumed that morning, unaware of the disdain and amusement he incited among the other track-goers, who proceeded to film him puking his guts out, snickering at how many views they would get by immortalizing him on TikTok. He decides to go back to Shanghai, and after some nights in a youth hostel spent by calling in some favours, he comes to take up lodging at a crummy, ground-floor flat near Anfu Lu in an Airbnb room managed by a former colleague of his at *TRIESTE* kind enough to help him out with a short-term lease, without a contract, pity-bargain and everything. He begins to sell off and give away his possessions which he no longer needs, leaving the items with no takers by the street for the trash collectors. He is ready to leave China anytime. This will be the final round of decluttering, he thinks.

The workless days start drifting into weeks. He visits cafés and bars and tea houses at random, sitting down all by himself and without a purpose, not making any effort to keep up appearances, his hair frizzy and unkempt, his beard scraggly in uneven patches, drawing the ire of some establishments for decreasing their customer turnover rate, and gaining the sympathy and reverence of proprietors who mistake him for some kind of an itinerant saint. He finds comfort in the familiarity of not having anything to do, the Southeast Asian way, as people in China like to put it. But there is no closure in this state of purposelessness. All this while, he is trying not to think of her, putting on a mask of reticence as he walks the streets of Xuhui to Changning, through to Hongkou to Pudong.

Out on a walk one late afternoon, he hears a constant murmuring behind him, but when he turns around to check for its source, all falls silent. The moment he looks ahead and moves on, the sound recommences, but this time it's louder, like a flurry of gibberish echoing down the streets. He looks back, and it is silent once more. This strange force coaxes him forward, an invisible collective of whispers bickering on and on endlessly. He goes forward, not paying any attention to the voices or attempting to discern the source of this seemingly infinite murmur. Each time a cessation of the muddled speech occurs, he is pulled back. But he must somehow propel himself to move on.

No time to pause for the gossip of the day, he thinks.

With the invisible murmur around him, it appears that the shadows tailing him are gone, one voice says.

No, that only appears so because the shadow has become a part of him, another voice replies.

Does he really not think of her? the first voice asks.

Can he really bring himself to forget? another voice wants to know.

He must forget.

But I cannot forget.

He will learn to forget.

I cannot yet forget.

He trudges on, imploring the streets and the city not to hold any grudges against the loutish pedestrian in loneliness, even if he were to spit, piss or shit across the archaic stone façades; he trusts them to withhold their judgement whether he acts as a revolutionary marching forward or a drunken hooligan hoping to subvert whatever comes in his way. The streets should be impartial to all that has happened throughout the course of history and be open to contingencies that will come to be after history, no matter how momentous or mundane the event.

He marches on unthinking as the streets keep talking about him. He approaches an unsighted piece of dog poo and planting his foot forward, he completely sinks his new sandal into it, turning it to slurry as he slides down the footpath like a footballer reaching for a tackle. The epic slide takes his front foot so far up into the air that he falls back, twisting his wrist to break his fall. He writhes in agony, clutching his wrist and then his ankle and then his back. As the pain subsides, he lifts his right sandal to see the brownish-green faeces wedged deep into the grooves of the outsole. He curses, then he laughs, but then he doesn't feel much of a difference between the two gestures any more. Miserably, he removes the sandal and starts to thwack it hard against the wretched world beneath him, trying to inflict some form of pain upon it, but only little loose bits of shit are sent flying in every direction, with the stickier pieces being driven in deeper between the rubber threads of the outsole.

He catches his breath and looks around. Isn't he now at Xujiahui park? The place of Luna and Rei's elaborate, bridal photoshoot? He gets up, but instead of swinging his sandal once more, he spits and stamps down on his spot of saliva.

Her, he must forget.

He gets back to Anfu Lu and stops in front of a signboard outside a gallery called BANK.

The signboard reads *Unquiet Heart Soliloquy*. That's the name of her exhibition, isn't it?

He descends the polished concrete stairs, and steps into a large gallery space with white walls and prefab, concrete flooring. Reminiscent of underground bunkers, the aesthetic of the space with its art-laden walls and track lights gives off an air of tasteful gentrification. He walks around, taking in the large, contrasty prints of experimental photography. Strangely, there isn't a soul to be seen in the entire gallery and he stands there utterly alone, not taking in or comprehending any of the artwork, but rather just in a state of awe at the sight of the sublime and beautiful objects on display: like a pair of brooding eyes cast in shadow that make him wonder who may be watching him now; or two Chinese ladies fighting over a Gucci bag, demonstrating a weird socioeconomic critique of culture and capitalism.

He comes to the other side of the display and at the centre he encounters a portrait of himself, with a void for a face, dragging on a cigarette, the headlights of a bus trailing away from him in the background. Stare as he might, it evokes nothing in him, no tug of the heart nor welling up in the eyes, because for him he cannot find a way into the picture, and for him there is no room to explore or establish any sort of emotional connection with the obscure portrait, a grainy mess of an exposure pushed too far in its development. At first, he thinks if this is indeed the centrepiece of the entire exhibition then it is a complete shame; but the force of the artwork compels him to stand in front of the picture for a little longer, this time as an observer and not a casual passer-by. Soon he will realize how foolish he is that he has misunderstood this intended discomfort towards him, because the picture is meant to unsettle its viewer, in its grotesque presentation of a face not having a face. This is not supposed to be him, but it is him at the same time, if he wants it to be, if he sees himself in that way. Can he not see it?

As he leaves, he sees the sponsor walking down the stairs towards the gallery, and the woman with raven-black hair and her sunglasses in late winter passes by him without so much as a glance in his direction. A draft blows in from outside, and he catches a whiff of her scent of incense, sandalwood, mixed with ink and asphalt, somehow reminding him of a time of normalcy in his life, and the goodness of more ordinary days. He stops halfway up the stairs and sensing his presence, she looks back in his direction.

'Do I know you?' she asks.

'Perhaps not,' he replies. 'I just wanted to say you smell fantastic, a little bit like Sappho actually,' he adds, no longer beset by trembling.

Spring Festival is approaching in a few weeks, and many of the shops throughout the city are already shuttered down, with the proprietors quickly leaving Shanghai to beat the annual mass migration home for the new year.

He gets off the train at Hailun Road and walks past the winding rivers until he reaches the 1933 Shanghai Slaughterhouse. For a moment he just stands at a distance from it, taking in the massive Gotham-Deco façade, its circular windows facing Sukhavati gleaming in the evening sun.

His every step up the Escheresque concrete staircase is accentuated by how silent it is around him. He climbs several long and twisty ramps on the way to her, only to be obstructed by a set of locked glass doors he gets there. It was on a poster at her exhibition that he chanced upon the name and location of her new studio; although it made no mention of its opening hours, he decided to try his luck anyway.

All he can do is wait. He waits while watching the sun set slowly over the western horizon.

Namo Amitābha, he whispers.

Sometime later, a young man shows up carrying a couple of Waimai takeaway boxes. He comes to a stop in front of the glass doors when he sees him.

'Is Gao Yuan Fei here?' he asks.

'Sorry I don't speak Mandarin that well,' he says with something of a French accent. 'Are you looking for Sofia?'

'Yes. Please tell her I'm no longer agnostic about love,' he tells him in English.

'Okay . . . just one moment,' he says, unlocking and disappearing through the tall, glass doors.

A few minutes later the young man returns, this time wearing a backpack and a cardigan, along with a takeaway box in hand.

'She'll be with you shortly,' he says, nodding to him in friendly acknowledgement as he knocks off for the day. 'Happy New Year, Mr Believer,' he says, heading down the ramp.

They spend a long time just watching the sky turn dark, listening to the faint roar of the city. She begins to cry. How could he have just abandoned her in Hangzhou? Why did he leave her to deal with everything all by herself?

He wraps his arms around her and holds her close, and as he kisses her head and runs his fingers through her long hair, he feels a great erection swelling up within his pants, but still he keeps their heads locked side by side in embrace, fearing that in the moment he looks into her eyes to tell her that he loves her, he would somehow lose everything again.

'I'm going on a train west to Kashgar. I want to know whether you will come with me,' he asks.

'To Xinjiang? But it's Germany I long for; have you forgotten already?'

'I haven't forgotten. We'll go to Germany too, taking turns to drive down the Autobahn all the way to the Nürburgring. But first, we'll ride the camels in Kashgar, the oasis will be our midpoint on the earth, and our new old Silk Road. What do you say?'

He waits for her answer, but for the longest time she doesn't say anything at all. They just continue to hang on to each other. There's nothing more she needs to say to convince him of her feelings for him. He feels that in place of the many impossible nights that they've been through, are myriad possibilities in each day ahead of them. In journeys as far as Kashgar to the Nürburgring, or as short as from the streets of Xuhui to the West Lake in Hangzhou, she's the only one he wants by his side. She is his only one in China.

Glossary

agak-agak	Malay for roughly or approximately.
ah neh	Tamil for elder brother.
baihua	Written vernacular Chinese.
baijiu	A colourless Chinese liquor usually distilled from fermented sorghum.
bak kut teh	Pork rib dish cooked in broth popularly served in Malaysia and Singapore where there is a predominant Hokkien and Teochew community. The name literally translates from the Hokkien dialect as 'meat bone tea'.
baozi	Steamed bun with meat or vegetable filling.
boba	Taiwanese drink of tea infused with milk or fruit and served over tapioca balls, called bubbles or boba.
cao ni ma	Expletive meaning 'fuck your mother'.
Chen Shimei	A Chinese opera character and epitome in China for a heartless and unfaithful man.
daigou	A form of cross-border exporting where an individual (the daigou), or a syndicated group of exporters outside China, purchases commodities on behalf of consumers in China. Daigou is a trust-based consumer-to-consumer system

that benefits the daigou with profits and the consumer with lower prices. Daigou may lead to unnecessary hoarding and stockpiling, causing certain goods like baby formula to be out of stock and unavailable to local residents within the exporting country.

diaohua chang Establishment providing singing performances for the Chinese community in Malaysia and Singapore, where a majority male crowd purchase flower garlands for the female singers as gratuity.

diaosi Chinese slang and Internet buzzword, first used in a sarcastic and self-deprecating manner to characterize males with mediocre looks and social standing. As diaosi went viral on the Internet, the term can also be used to describe the ordinary Chinese citizen facing everyday struggles. Diaosi literally **means 'dick hair'.**

doujiang A fresh soy milk in Chinese cuisine. It can be served hot or cool, sweet or savoury.

erhua Phonological process of adding a r-colouring to the *er* syllables in spoken Mandarin Chinese, most common in Northern-Chinese dialects.

full died Exaggerated expression, of being so full that one is approaching death.

ganbei Ganbei means 'dry-cup', or to drink a toast, in Mandarin Chinese. In professional and business settings, the more you drink, the more respect you show to the other party.

guanxi	A personal trust and a strong relationship with someone, that can involve moral obligations and exchanging favours.
guobier	Thin pieces of deep fried dough contained in jianbing.
huaqiao	An individual or people of Chinese nationality residing outside of China.
huaren	An individual or people of Chinese ethnicity.
heng ah huat ah	Hokkien traditional festive expression wishing one luck and prosperity.
izakaya	Informal Japanese bar that serves alcoholic drinks and snacks. Izakaya are casual places for after-work drinking, similar to a pub, a Spanish tapas bar, or an American saloon or tavern.
jianbing	Traditional Chinese street food similar to crêpes.
jingbo	A concussion idiophone of the cymbal type of the Han Chinese, with the prefix 'jing' denoting its regional affiliation to Beijing and primary usage within Beijing opera.
jinghu	A bowed, spike-lute chordophone of the Han Chinese, used primarily in Beijing opera.
Jingxi	The opera of the capital, or Beijing opera.
jitong	A spirit medium or shaman who practises Chinese folk religion, also tongji.
jiu huang da di huat ah huat	Luck and prosperity to the Nine. Emperor Gods.
kopi-o	Traditional Nanyang coffee served with sugar and without milk.
laoban	Boss.

laojia   The old familial home a Chinese family
                    originates from.

laowai   A foreigner in mainland China or Taiwan,
                    particularly a Western one.

Lao Gan Ma   a brand of chilli sauces made in China,
                    credited with popularising Chinese
                    chilli oil in the western world. Lao Gan
                    Ma literally means Old Godmother.

liang ban mian Cold mixed noodles.

lilong   Unique architectural product of
                    Shanghai, a cross between an English
                    terrace-house and the traditional Chinese
                    courtyard.

Li Sao   Ancient Chinese poem from the 3rd
                    century BCE attributed to Qu Yuan,
                    purported to be his biography. The literal
                    meaning of Li Sao is not a straightforward
                    one, it can be taken to mean *encountering
                    sorrow* or *leaving with sorrow*.

Lizu   Kra-Dai speaking ethnic group, the
                    largest minority ethnic group on
                    Hainan Island.

longjingcha   A variety of pan-roasted green tea from
                    the area of Longjing Village in Hangzhou,
                    Zhejiang Province, China. Longjingcha
                    literally translates as 'Dragon Well tea'.

luogudianzi   Gong and drum rhythmic patterns in
                    Beijing opera.

mamak   Indoor and open-air food establishments
                    in Southeast Asia, mainly in the countries
                    of Malaysia especially and also
                    Singapore, which serve a type of Indian
                    Muslim cuisine unique to the region by
                    its Indian community.

mei po	Chinese matchmaker.
Namo Amitābha	Homage to the Amitābha Buddha.
nasi lemak	A dish originating in Malay cuisine consisting of fragrant rice cooked in coconut milk and pandan leaf.
paiban	A concussion idiophone of the Han Chinese used in the percussion section of the Beijing opera ensemble, made of three long rectangular blocks of hardwood with one block being slightly thicker than the other two, *pai* means to strike, while *ban* means flat board.
pianerchuan	Noodle soup dish from Hangzhou, made with sliced pork fried in lard, sliced bamboo shoots, soy sauce and pickled Chinese cabbage.
Qin Xianglian	Wife of Chen Shimei. Chen betrays her after he becomes an official in the imperial city and subsequently marries the Emperor's sister. Xianglian is translated literally as fragrant lotus.
rokok	Bahasa for cigarette.
shabi	Stupid cunt.
shushu	Chinese for uncle.
steng	Derived from the Malay word *setengah*, steng is slang for the sharing of one cigarette.
Tantan	A Chinese mobile dating app.
teh tarik	Hot milk tea beverage found in Southeast Asia, prepared by 'pulling' a strong brew of black tea with condensed milk back and forth repeatedly between two containers to produce a thick foam.

warung	A wide category of small businesses, either in the form of a small retail shop or eatery, found in Indonesia and Malaysia.
weishang	Chinese micro retailers.
wenyanwen	Classical Chinese.
xiaogege	A cute term of address for a young man.
xiaolongbao	A type of small Chinese steamed bun (baozi) traditionally prepared in a small bamboo steaming basket (xiaolong).
xiaoluo	A small metal gong idiophone of the Han Chinese, played together with another bigger gong (*daluo*) in Beijing opera.
xungen	Cultural and literary movement emphasizing the reconstruction of identity and appreciation of culture, literally meaning to search for one's roots.
yakitori	Japanese grilled chicken skewers made from bite sized pieces of meat from all different parts of the chicken, such as the breasts, thighs, skin, liver and other innards.
yanjiudian	A Chinese tobacco and alcohol shop.
youtiao	A long deep-fried strip of dough that is lightly salted and made so they can be torn lengthwise in two.
yinyang pot	Chinese hot pot made of steel, with compartments in the shape of the philosophical concept of yin and yang.
Zhonghua minzu	Modern political term used to form a Chinese nationality that transcends ethnic divisions.